COUNTRY HOUSE CHRISTMAS MURDER

Berkshires Cozy Mystery

ANDREA KRESS

❀ Created with Vellum

Chapter One

Is there anything more gorgeous than fall in the Berkshire Mountains?

Not the hot, last gasp of Indian Summer, nor the dreary rain and cloudy days that inevitably follow. I'm talking about those glorious crisp yet sunny days in October when every deciduous tree has burst into a show of distinct colors so that from a distance it seems an impossible tapestry of red, orange and yellow with the counterpoint of green from the pines.

The days were shorter, the nights were cold, but the sheer explosion of color that hit me each morning as I looked out my window toward the woods instantly put me in a good mood. Although I had reason to be in the best of humor. Here was I, Aggie Burnside, still in West Adams, Massachusetts, a small town in the Berkshires, renting a room from Miss Manley, a sharp and thoughtful older woman who provided me with meals, conversation and advice. I might think of myself as a full-blown adult, but I was less than half a year out of nurses' training and working for the handsome and thoughtful Doctor John Taylor. My earlier ambition of working in the hospital where I trained in New York City had been sidelined by what appeared to be a short-term, part-time position that turned into a permanent full-time job experiencing the gamut of health cases in the two towns where he divided his practice. Unlike the City's hospitals, we didn't see an intentional gunshot or knife wound, but there were plenty of farm accidents that could be just as gory and lethal, especially because those stoic men waited until their wives demanded they see the doctor when they couldn't get up to work. There were the usual childhood diseases, although I expect I'll see more of them next spring when outbreaks such as measles and chickenpox tend to occur. But the bread and butter of the practice was a result of the broken limbs and chronic ailments originating from the hardworking lives of the residents of the area.

My time was usually spent in the adjacent town of Adams, just up the road, a booming town where my employer had acquired the practice of the retired Doctor Mitchell. In the afternoon, John and I would drive back to West Adams for office hours and, since the distance was nominal, any potential patient who missed him at one location knew where to find him at the other. Although he had hospital privileges in Pittsfield, the nearest city, he had very little need of their services so far in my time working with him.

That particular day, I was able to sleep in and wear my civilian clothes—as I usually wore my nurse's uniform for work—since John had been attending a conference in Boston for the past few days. I was envious of his trip because I had cousins there whom I hadn't seen for some time and there was so much to see and do. Though I stopped in the West Adams office each day to do paperwork and answer the phones, he had let enough people know that he would be gone to preclude anyone's pounding on the door and going away frustrated. He had looked forward to this interruption in his usual routine and I didn't mind the break, either, especially since he would be back Friday evening and there was an entire weekend ahead for casual activities—long walks in the woods, leaf-peeping as the locals called it, perhaps a dinner out or a movie in Adams.

John got back in the late afternoon, bursting through the office door as I sat at the reception desk, sorting through the mail.

"Aggie! Hello, how nice to be back!"

He swept in, gave me a hug and a kiss on the cheek, his face ruddy from driving with the windows down.

I laughed at his enthusiasm and the sheer pleasure of seeing him again.

He plopped his suitcase on the floor and looking around, smiled broadly.

"I gather it was a successful meeting?" I asked.

"Oh, yes. Wonderful! Except for the last bit. The luncheon and the business meeting of discussing one motion or another. Ugh! That's not for me. But the camaraderie was tremendous, and I got to meet some physicians I have heard about or talked to on the telephone for an inquiry or a referral. They were all so welcoming."

"And did you have some fantastic meals? And see the sights?"

"I've seen the sights so many times, I didn't do any touring. There were too many interesting papers and presentations to listen to. I did have a lobster dinner one night, however. Ah, I love being here in the mountains, but lobster...."

I had to laugh because I understood his longing perfectly.

"When we visit my aunt and uncle in Boston, that is the first thing we ask for," I said.

"Anything exciting happen here?"

"Not a thing. You have only been gone a few days, you know. No emergencies, knock wood," I said, rapping my hand on the desk for emphasis. The few requests for appointments have been pushed into next week. So, you have a nice quiet weekend ahead."

"I hope it's not entirely quiet. Surely we can go see a movie tomorrow?"

"That would be wonderful." I stood to gather the papers in a neat pile in front of me.

"I didn't tell you that one of my classmates from medical school was there. Fred Browne. Lovely man. He's got a roaring practice in

Cambridge. We had a great time catching up and then he told me his mother lives in this neck of the woods, as he put it. Actually, over the border in Vermont."

"That's a fairly remote area. Did he grow up there?"

"Mostly in Boston but their summer place was out here. He called it Browne's Castle."

"Was he pulling your leg?"

"I'm not sure, but we'll find out tomorrow if you're game."

"What do you mean?"

"Do you have other plans?" he asked teasingly.

"You know my curiosity is greater than any obligation I may have had."

He took my hands in his. "I have been asked by Fred to look in on his mother, who is an eccentric old bird. An author, somewhat of a recluse, and now he says perhaps aside from heart issues, she's in some kind of mental decline."

I'm sure I looked alarmed, wondering what he meant by that phrase.

"Nothing dangerous, I assure you. He said that the last time he spoke to her she said she was sure someone was going to kill her."

"Why?"

"When we go tomorrow, perhaps we'll find out."

Chapter Two

I was having dinner at Miss Manley's tonight instead of with John, who was exhausted from the conference and the long drive back from Boston. As the weather was getting colder, Annie, the maid who was also an accomplished cook, had switched from the lighter fare of the summer to savory dishes like baked beans, ham and brown bread or stew with biscuits. As I walked across the back garden from John's house, I could smell that night's offering of corned beef and cabbage before I even came in the kitchen door and looked forward to a cup of strong coffee to take the chill off. Annie's habit was to make the dinner and then go home to her own family, leaving us to eat at our leisure and clean up afterward. She was just getting her hat and coat when I inhaled appreciatively.

"That smells marvelous."

"The way you go on about my cooking makes me wonder what sort of food you grew up with," she said, buttoning the wool coat up toward her neck. She looked me over from head to toe, not for the first time, taking in the fact that I was tall and thin. I hoped she didn't think I had been underfed as a child.

"My mother is an excellent cook, but she would rather be reading than working in the kitchen so I would say her cuisine was geared to dishes that didn't need a lot of attention. Roasts or chops, for example."

"Those need just as much attention as a stew," she said. "The timing is everything."

I said goodnight to her while remembering my mother seated at the kitchen table, either reading a novel or a magazine with one eye on the dinner in progress. The real difference between her and Annie was that my mother cooked out of necessity while Annie did it as an act of artistry. Although she was unmarried and lived with her elderly parents and younger brother in town, I believe she walked home and most likely started a second meal for the family. That was the life of women, I had learned, and I was happy that I was young, single and earning my way for the time being.

While we ate, I told Miss Manley of my impending visit the next day and mentioned that the house was called Browne's Castle.

She hooted with laughter when I told her that. "I think you will enjoy yourself. Although I have not been there, I've heard that Mr. and Mrs. Browne created quite an impressive abode. I won't say anything more—I don't want to spoil your experience."

"I hope there isn't a moat or a dungeon."

"I will say no more," she said, her eyes twinkling. "Did Doctor Taylor have a satisfactory conference?"

"It seems so. I hadn't given it much thought before, but he probably misses the camaraderie of other doctors since he is one of very few in this area. I would hate for him to think of himself as 'only a country doctor.' He is so much more than that. Even though I work rather regular hours Monday through Friday, I know that he takes calls on the weekend and even gets called out to the more remote farms."

"Yes, he is a dedicated man," Miss Manley commented. "We are lucky to have him."

* * *

After a Saturday morning of minor errands—post office to mail letters to family and friends, butcher to pick up meat for Sunday dinner—and a quick sandwich for lunch, I headed to John's house through the Lewises' back garden, around the side of the house and into his backyard and then the side door that opened to his office. The door was unlocked and the reception area was empty, the door closed to the living quarters of his house. He must have heard me come in and popped his head around the corner from the kitchen as I stood briefly sorting through the mail that had arrived.

John held up his finger, indicating he had his mouth full before speaking.

"Take your time," I said. "I'll just open these and see what's what."

He ducked back into his kitchen leaving the door open and I saw him sit before a plate of sandwiches and a glass of milk.

"It looks like Mr. Russell has finally caught up with the invoices I sent him." I flapped a five-dollar bill in the air in triumph.

He raised his eyebrows in appreciation. "Not bad. Say, did you used to work for a loan shark in New York?"

"Loan sharks make their money off inflated interest rates. You don't change any interest at all. But we could change that." At his widened eyes I had to add, "Just kidding."

He pointed to an unfolded map on the other side of the table. "We're going due north through North Adams into Vermont and then the directions get a bit tricky." He pointed to an area on the map that showed a vast area of green without any towns or roads. Unfolding a paper, he read: "Thirty miles past Stamford, turn left onto a graveled road. These are Fred's directions. Continue west and go left at the first fork in the road, right at the second and left at the third. The house is at the end of the road. If we have any problems finding it, her man, Bruce Mowbray, will come looking for us."

"That sounds simple enough," I said doubtfully. "Have you ever been in that area?"

"I've been to Vermont, of course, skiing, but not rambling around the countryside."

"Let's hope it's not a wild goose chase. You do have a spare tire?"

He gave me a look that said I shouldn't have asked.

"Better safe than sorry." Oh, dear. I was beginning to sound like my mother.

It was a pleasant drive on that cloudy day to Adams and then through North Adams, which I hadn't seen in a while. A large town at the confluence of two rivers, it seemed very prosperous and, as we drove through the old residential neighborhood, quite elegant.

"This has been a mill town from when it was first founded, initially lumber and then moving into textiles, shoes and gloves," John said.

"Do you know there is a town in New York State called Gloversville? Our family took a vacation and drove through the Mohawk Valley—that's where it is. It was the center of glove production in this country, my father said."

"Factory girls. Sometime in the last century, young women and probably children, too, were drawn to such places from their family farms to work in the factories. Grinding work, I imagine, but it was a paycheck."

I looked out over the valley, the autumn display of foliage in stark contrast to the chimneys of the factories that sprang up in the distance.

"You know, everyone thinks of New York City as such a glamorous place, but it has a lot of industry and factories, too."

"I haven't spent much time in the City," John said. "Mostly Boston."

"Well, you'll just have to come down for Thanksgiving at the end of next month. My parents would like to meet you and we can explore Manhattan." My heart was beating a bit fast at my bold invitation.

He turned to smile at me. "I would like that. From what you've said, your parents sound like wonderful people."

"Yes," I said. "They are." Images swept across my mind of showing John our sleepy suburban Pelham, then the excitement of Manhattan—maybe we could have a meal there and see a Broadway show! Then, a down-home Thanksgiving dinner at which my mother excelled. Something wonderful to look forward to.

We continued north past Clarksburg and, shortly thereafter, we crossed the Vermont State line.

"Stamford should be coming along very soon and then we are supposed to pay attention to how far we've come so as not to miss the turnoff," I said.

"Yes, skipper," he said, saluting me.

Stamford was a rather small town, and we were past it in a blink of the eye. Then just road and endless forest on both sides and not much traffic.

"Gosh, this is remote," I said. "Do you suppose Fred's mother lives out here by herself?"

"Perhaps this Mowbray fellow takes care of it when she's not here. Fred said this was their summer place and I'm surprised she is here this late in the season. Even though it's pleasant enough today, you know how the weather can turn in a moment."

Looking down at the sheet of directions, I also kept an eye on the odometer as we passed a few ancient wooden barns no longer in use, one beginning to lean and likely due to collapse in the season's first heavy snowstorm. Finally, a driveway could be seen leading to a farmhouse in a clearing, but that was the only habitation until we got to the thirty-mile point and John slowed the car as we looked for an opening in the woods.

"There." I pointed to a wide breach in the foliage set off on each side by a low stone marker providing an unobtrusive entryway that somebody did not wish to proclaim too obviously. The first hundred feet felt somewhat paved but then the surface became earth scattered with gravel that deteriorated to a rock-strewn dirt road.

"Hold on to your hat!" John said, but I was already hanging onto the strap on the passenger side as we were jostled from side to side with the rocking of the car. John slowed as he dodged a boulder.

"How in the world could someone drive out here at night? It's dark enough in the middle of the day."

We continued carefully with both of us leaning forward to watch for any other impediments in the way until we came to the first fork in the road and went left, as directed, to a path that was wider and more carefully graded.

"Look! There's something there," I said. "I think it was a bear!"

John stepped on the brakes and looked to where I pointed.

"It bent down out of sight almost as soon as I saw it."

We waited with the motor running and heard and saw nothing else, so proceeded slowly onward. There were occasional breaks in the deep forest that surrounded us where low-lying meadows could be seen and a glimpse of a deer staring at us.

"Right at the next fork," I read aloud.

On we went across the smooth yet unpaved surface for perhaps a half a mile. Again, I could not imagine trying to drive in or out on a muddy spring day or after a snowstorm. The next divergence was to the right and came up suddenly with the path wide, the trees less dense, and we found ourselves looking down into a long, densely wooded valley with the turrets of an enormous imposing structure of dark red sandstone sticking up. All that John and I could do was stare before he burst out laughing.

After he wiped his eyes, he continued, "Fred was so strange when he first mentioned that I visit and seemed embarrassed when he said people called it Browne's Castle. But now I know why."

"Well, perhaps there is a moat after all."

From our perspective, although we could not see the ground floor, we could see four round, crenelated towers, three of them probably the height of the two-story building while the fourth tower was one tier higher.

"What a wonderful view of the valley they must have from up there," I said, imagining myself walking on the roof, then wondering if it was accessible from the house and how high the balustrade was.

"Of course, a real castle would never have those mature trees obscuring the impending attackers or the view of the defenders." John said, putting the car in low gear, and we descended the winding road downward, feeling the air even cooler here than in the shade of the forest above.

"What an extraordinary place," I said as we drew closer and pulled up in front of the building. With the engine turned off, the only sounds were birdsong and the wind rustling the yellow leaves of the beeches whose arms spread wide across the broad lawn.

"The landscaping is exquisite," I commented, noting the manicured plantings bright with the last of the season's chrysanthemums.

We got out and I had the silly notion that one didn't just go up to the front and ring a doorbell to a castle, but how else could someone know we were here? Shout halloo? I looked up at the towers half expecting to see archers peering down at us, bows strung in anticipation of the attack. Instead, the reality was a tall, gaunt, older man in a flannel shirt who opened the massive front door and approached us. His craggy face displayed years outside in sun, wind and likely freezing weather, but his stoic expression indicated he would not be fazed by what came his way. A true Yankee.

"Missus has been expecting you," he said, nodding toward the house with a jerk of his head.

We followed him through the doorway into a dark foyer that opened to a vast room, two stories high, which occupied a good portion of the area of the ground floor. We gaped at the immense size of the space while the man disappeared through a distant archway, ducking his head as he went.

John whistled in appreciation, pushed his hat back on his head and with hands on his hips surveyed the astonishing scene.

Across from us was a colossal fireplace, large enough for a person to walk into—actually several people—topped by a carved wooden mantel supported by marble columns. The andirons inside the hearth were several feet high, large enough to support a tree trunk, which is what would be needed to heat a room of that size. Far above the fire-place was a soaring mullioned window that illuminated the entire room with natural light even on this overcast October day.

The wood-paneled walls on either side of the hearth reached to an incised plaster ceiling but the most remarkable thing was the artful symmetrical display of weaponry, one cluster of swords positioned to form a star shape, another forming a succession of inverted Vs. There were guns, pistols, swords, spears, pikes, spears, halberds and maces in careful geometric arrangements. And that was only two of the walls of the room!

Turning to my right, the armory was replaced by portraits of men in varying degrees of plaid, posed on rocks with craggy scenery and ferocious-looking clouds in the background while the few paintings of women were demure in their powdered wigs and stylized 18th century interiors. Up above these portraits was a wooden balcony, which ranged across three walls along with openings to rooms beyond, but whose staircase was not visible from this room.

Our rapture was interrupted by a chuckle from one of the arch-ways, and out stepped a stylish older woman, her hair still a youthful brown, smiling brightly at our childish wonderment.

"Everybody who sees this for the first time has the same reaction, my dear," she said to me, noting my embarrassment. "I'm Hextilda Cumming Browne," she said, extending a hand and shaking mine warmly.

"Agnes Burnside," I replied.

"A Burns!" she said.

"No, Burnside," I corrected her.

"I always know a fellow Scot when I see one," she said, winking and turning to her other guest. "And you must be John Taylor. Fred-erick has spoken of you so many times." She continued to hold his hand and sighed before letting go.

"I hope you didn't have any trouble finding us."

"No," I said, "but I think I saw a bear in the woods."

She laughed. "I don't think there has been a bear around here in years. You may have seen a vagrant or hobo. Some men have taken to foraging in the woods and here we don't prosecute for poaching."

"This is quite a collection," John said, looking around. "I hope you are not anticipating a siege anytime soon."

"Our clan has been through a lot over the centuries but thankfully things have been calm so far on this side of the pond."

She had no trace of a Scottish accent, which made me wonder if she was an American who married a Scot or if her family came to New England from Europe and brought the extensive arsenal with them. Or was hers a rich American family that purchased history and the accouterments from some impoverished laird more than happy to get rid of the no longer functional weapons? Her vague comment begged for clarification, and I was not disappointed.

"How long have you been here?"

She looked at her wristwatch and said, "About five minutes, I would guess." She put her hand on my arm as if to reassure me that her teasing was just that.

"My family is descended from the Comyn clan, once a powerful group defeated by Robert the Bruce. Yes, the one Scot that most people seem to know and deify. But mark my words, he was brutal, and we've never recovered from the loss of land and standing."

"Yet...?" John said, holding his arms out as if to counter her statement.

"In Scotland, that is. My late husband did very well in business and as a nod to me, his architect found several buildings in disrepair and had the pieces shipped to the States and reassembled here. The exterior was the collaboration of the architect, the builder and my husband, designed to contain both the old, wonderful, reconstructed rooms as well as the modern ones for our use. Clever, don't you think?"

"Brilliant," I marveled at the notion, the effort and the expense of executing the plan.

She led us through an archway into a long hall and insisted we see the view from her study. We complied and found in that room facing the same direction as the window in the Great Hall a mullioned clerestory running the length of the wall illuminating the huge area. There were two desks, back to back in the middle of a large Persian carpet, like partners' desks in my father's old-fashioned law office. One wall consisted of rows of books with a rolling ladder allowing access to the highest shelf and, despite the tidy order of the majority of the room, there were pages scattered on the floor next to both of the desks.

"My filing system," she laughed. "We switch desks back and forth as I make a mess. Then my secretary, Adele, will put everything in order before the end of the day. We're just finishing up the first draft."

My look of inquiry was met by her slight arch of eyebrows. "Didn't Fred tell you?

I write romance novels, bodice-rippers they sometimes call them. My hero is a Highlander, of course. What else could he be?" This set her off laughing.

"I didn't know," I said.

"No, Fred had never mentioned it to me," John added.

"I'm not surprised. Probably a little bit embarrassed. Although it did help pay the medical school bills. Anyway, romance novels are not everyone's cup of tea." She busied herself shuffling through some papers on the larger desk.

"I just got through with nurses' training this past June and certainly didn't have much time for pleasure reading, that's for sure." It sounded like a weak excuse even to me.

"Never mind. Here, this is what I was looking for." She held out a creased piece of paper to John, who opened it carefully, then looked up in surprise.

"Have the police seen this?" he asked.

"Go ahead, show Miss Burns. I'm sure she's dying to know what it is." As she smiled, I saw her twin set matched the teal blue of her eyes regarding me with mischief. Of course, I obliged and looked over at the crudely written note.

You will die.

"Now how stupid is that? Obviously, I'm going to die sometime, as does everyone. You would think he might come up with something a little more ominous, such as, 'Tomorrow you will die,' or 'Beware the Ides of November,' or at least a bit of doggerel. No offense to Robbie Burns, my dear," she said in my direction.

"Don't you think this is serious?" I asked.

"Really, Mrs. Browne, you ought to have called the police. Not have a country doctor such as I as your counselor in a criminal matter."

"At first I thought it was some disgruntled reader. As I said, romance is not for everyone. And if I am correct, this is a man's handwriting, or someone pretending to be a man, no offense, Doctor Taylor." John was taken aback by her comment, but she went on. "I then realized that it might be something more and I did call the police. You can imagine what happened then. We are in a small county here with limited resources and they sent one of the two available deputies, I don't know. Up to my front door came the actual sheriff in his everyday flannel shirt and farm boots. It was quite a disappointment. I had hoped it would be some handsome rogue who could be the second lead in my book, you know, to tempt the heroine away—even temporarily—from our beloved hero. This one didn't do the trick, however." She allowed herself a good laugh.

"Let's go into tea, and I'll continue," she said.

John and I exchanged looks, whether it was the sudden change of subject or in my case the notion of having such a conversation with my mother, I couldn't say, but we followed her to one corner of the room where a round table was set for tea.

"I showed him the note and he ran his hand through his mop of hair. Surprisingly he had exquisite hands, albeit with dirt under the fingernails."

John cleared his throat. "And what did he do about your report?"

Hextilda shook her head as if coming out of a reverie. "Nothing. He did have the sense to copy the words onto another piece of paper. At my urging." She laughed at this and reached for the teapot. "I can't imagine what he intended to do with it. Cream or sugar?"

I could see her writer's brain at work relating the description of the man, noting everything about him and imbuing him with some quality that would work well with her plot. Too bad it wasn't the perpetrator of the note whom she described since the level of detail was so acute.

"You must have some of Eleanor's scones, they are the best," she continued.

Although we had had lunch only a few hours earlier, the three-tiered tray loaded with scones, palmiers, shortbread and chocolate wafers was too tempting to refuse and I took one of each. As I ate, she told us of her long writing career, her decision to slow down as she was getting older although her fans pestered her for more.

"I could probably do this forever, but my children are starting to get after me about it. First, they don't want me to be here as late in the season as I stay. But what is the point of having a home such as this except that it gives the quiet and isolation needed to write? Boston is exciting, but there are so many social engagements and family to see that I never get as much done there."

"Is Fred your only child?" I asked.

"There's Allan, my eldest, who is a stockbroker. Then Frederick, who you've met already. And Caroline, the youngest, who runs an art gallery in New York. Awful stuff, but people seem to like it. You'll meet them soon enough." She left it at that, and we chatted about West Adams and John's practice, all the while keeping an eye on the darkening sky, which could portend a storm and a muddy road out to the main road.

As we said goodbye at the door, she asked John how long until we were back home, and he gave a reasonable estimate, wondering why she had asked. She gave us each a kiss on the cheek and wished us well, smiling in a mischievous way.

We marveled all the way home about the extraordinary house and our quirky hostess, who had been entertaining, funny and baffling at turns. John found it hard to reconcile her personality with that of her son, whom he had known so long as a straightforward scientist and doctor, but we agreed that there were always anomalies in families; it was what made the world so interesting.

Hardly two steps back into the office in West Adams, the telephone rang. John picked up the receiver and seemed surprised, then puzzled, then pleased. He thanked the caller profusely and laughed.

"That was Mrs. Browne. She's invited us for a Christmas weekend."

"Oh, no, John. We were going to be with my family in Pelham, remember?"

He came close and put his arms around me. "She said a Christmas weekend. Not *the* Christmas weekend."

I had the same puzzled look on my face that he had just a few minutes earlier.

"What does that mean?"

"She said she found December 25 profoundly sad and decided to create a Christmas-like weekend at the Castle earlier in the month. And we're invited. Christmas tree, festive food, something called a Dundee cake. No smoking, however."

I thought it was the oddest thing I had heard in a long time. We barely knew the woman.

"Come on, it will be fun!" John said.

"Ho, ho, ho," I replied.

Chapter Three

S tuart, Miss Manley's nephew, and his wife Glenda, my
former classmate at nurses' training, came up for a weekend
in mid-November, prompting Annie's customary grumble
about having to get their room ready. No one entered the room when
they weren't there, so I was sure there was minimal cleaning or
dusting to be done but she crashed around, moving the furniture and
bashing the broom into the corners followed by a ritual vacuuming.

I thought it was a strange time for them to leave New York City
with all the holiday cultural offerings while West Adams' charms at
this time of year were the end of the leaf-peeping season, the beginning of the cold drizzle with sodden leaves everywhere. They had
already invited Miss Manley to their place in the City for Thanksgiving, only two weeks away, but perhaps they had some last-minute
planning to accomplish or just needed a respite from their urban life.

Glenda breezed in the kitchen door with pink cheeks, a broad
smile and a large maternity dress that swamped her small frame. She
gave Annie a hug and kiss, which alarmed the woman, and then
embraced me as well. She smelled of cold weather and a hint of some
new perfume, but she was definitely blooming as people like to

describe pregnant women. Stuart had on his usual distracted look as if not knowing what he was doing in this kitchen in this small town until he saw his aunt enter the room and then he beamed his most charming smile.

"How good to see you," Miss Manley said, embracing him and patting down the upturned collar of his overcoat.

Stuart never quite knew how to greet me. A handshake was too formal, a hug and kiss too familiar, so he settled for a kiss on each cheek a la française.

There was the usual commotion of inquiring about the trip, had they eaten yet, where were their bags, and Stuart went out again to retrieve them from his Packard in the driveway.

"It's so cold!" Glenda commented.

Miss Manley had to laugh. "Dear, you grew up next door and I can remember you playing out in the snow for hours without complaint. It was your mother who made you come in before frostbite took over."

"I guess I'm too used to the City. And our apartment has the most wonderful steam heat. I don't even put a sweater on when I'm at home." She looked around trying to familiarize herself with the heating arrangements in Miss Manley's house, but in the kitchen, the only source of heat was the large stove. There was a large boiler in the basement fed by coal from the man who did yard work and other odd jobs, and it was only Miss Manley's frugality that made the house chillier than it needed to be.

She shepherded us into the sitting room where a fire was providing additional warmth to the room and Glenda stood before it, still in her overcoat, warming her hands.

"Come, sit down, dear," Miss Manley said to her from the couch. "I've just finished knitting a lap robe for you to wear in the car on your way home, but it looks as though you could use it now."

Glenda laughed at how silly she must seem but took off her coat and gratefully draped the deep blue afghan across her legs and sighed. "So nice to be here," she said, almost purring.

Stuart was dragging their usual overabundance of luggage upstairs while Glenda called out to him to bring back the 'you-know-what.' She was referring to the gin and didn't want Annie, a teetotaler and rule abider in this time of Prohibition although the maid knew quite well what went on in the sitting room and turned a blind eye, to know.

I was looking forward to a chatty cocktail party of the kind we used to have in the garden in warmer weather and Stuart did not disappoint, bringing a quart of unlabeled clear alcohol and a jar of olives. Glenda clapped in anticipation, and we began to talk about old classmates while Stuart disappeared into the kitchen for glasses and ice. It was surprising that she ran into so many of the girls in a place as large as New York, but they seemed to frequent the same places by force of habit, whether it was Macy's or a particular lunch counter.

"How is business?" I asked him as he fixed the drinks for us.

"Smashing, actually. I've spent the last month traipsing around to every bookstore in the City with my little display cart of our books and the new line of boys' action series. Everyone has expressed tremendous interest in those books. Just think of it, you go into a bookstore looking for something for yourself or a gift for a friend and there in front of you is just the thing for your young nephew! I believe they are priced competitively, and the covers are attractive."

"I just hope they sell," Glenda commented. She had become increasingly pessimistic about money after getting married, having spent her girlhood in relative wealth and her subsequent years oblivious about financial matters until her mother died.

Stuart patted her on the head and smiled. "Don't worry. We'll make a killing. Everyone likes to read."

"Aggie, Miss Manley, you should see what the Depression has done to people. There are men on street corners selling apples for a nickel. Can you imagine? Some of them are dressed in faded business suits and you can almost picture them two years ago as wealthy Wall Street bankers. There are hobos sleeping in the parks, too. It's awful."

"Now, now, honey bun. Don't be all doom and gloom. We'll get out of this mess soon enough, I'll bet." He turned to me. "Do you know that CR, Cash Ridley," he clarified to his aunt, "really did come through on investing in Hudson-Manley and has been a tremendous booster of the business. He's introduced me to I don't know how many important people and there may be more interest in the future." I was sure people were impressed by Stuart and his Ivy League look, with curly blond hair and optimistic attitude, although the ascot he habitually wore was a silly affectation in my opinion.

"Chin chin, everyone," he said, and we raised our glasses in a toast at being together once again in the presence of Miss Manley, the smell of the roast wafting in from the kitchen, and a hefty quart of alcohol at our disposal.

"Speaking of books, John and I had the opportunity to meet Hextilda Cumming Browne," I said.

"Oh, really," Glenda said. "I love her books."

Stuart's eyes widened and he tried not to roll them upwards in astonishment.

"Darling, they are hardly literature," he said.

"I know, that's why I like them." She stifled a giggle.

Miss Manley was a bit baffled by the exchange. "Aggie, you told me a bit about her and her home, but I don't think I understand what sort of books she writes."

"They're romance novels in a historical setting," Glenda said loftily.

"They call them bodice-rippers in the trade," Stuart said.

Miss Manley raised her eyebrows but said nothing.

"They're fun. It's about a beautiful maiden who falls in love with a Scottish rogue somewhere back in time," Glenda said.

"Eighteenth century," said Stuart.

"Yes, with kilts and castles and stern parents who don't understand true love."

"She seems to have a long-running series," I said. "How do you keep the tension of unrequited love going through so many books?"

"You'd be surprised," Glenda said.

"Actually, not so well. How many sighs can a heroine emit without it being boring?"

Glenda tapped him on the arm in annoyance.

"How many assignations can the couple have? I would imagine after the eighth book any sensible reader would scream, 'Marry her for God's sake!'"

Miss Manley laughed long and hard at this assessment.

"Well, I can tell you this. Her publisher has seen the sales declining, whether due to the horrible economic crisis we are in with her readers unable to afford her books or lack of interest in such stuff," he said.

"You would think in hard times that people would gravitate toward more fantastical literature...," I said.

"Hardly literature."

"All right, more fantastical works," I corrected myself. "Haven't you seen an interest in less realistic themes?"

"Interesting concept, Aggie. There should be more interest, and perhaps we need to look at presenting those works to people as a means of escape from the harsh realities of life." He looked down and was deep in thought about what I had suggested.

"But even so, I think they are tired of Hextilda Cumming Browne." He said this in an affected voice.

"I can't comment on her literary qualities since I haven't read any of her books, but I shall try at least one. The thing is, she is an incredibly interesting person and lives in the most extraordinary house—a castle really—and she has invited John and me for a weekend next month."

Now I had captured Stuart's unerring interest in all things social and social climbing, if I'm not being too harsh. He lived for society gossip, longed to hang out with the wealthy and important and was somewhat annoyed that I, who cared not for class distinctions, 'names,' or people who were au courant, should be invited to a weekend at a famous author's home.

"How did that happen?" he asked. It was almost an accusation.

"John went to medical school with her son Frederick, and knowing we were fairly close to where she lived, he asked us to look in on her.

"Where does she live?" He seemed annoyed that such a personage, one whom he had disparaged earlier, was in proximity to his aunt's home and no one had told him.

"She lives in southern Vermont, in the middle of nowhere."

"That doesn't sound like fun at all," Glenda said.

"It's a beautiful location and an amazing home. Her late husband took the innards of several old houses or castles in Scotland and had them reassembled here in the States."

"Oh, *that* Browne," Stuart said, snapping his fingers as he realized to whom I referred and brightening. He was not to let any important social connection escape his notice.

"Swords and pistols line the walls. Ancient portraits of I don't know who, a stuffed deer in one of the rooms."

"Ugh," Glenda said.

"Dinner's ready," Annie announced from the doorway, her coat slung over her arm before departing.

I was glad I did not reveal why we had been asked to check in on her or the crude threatening note she had pretended to ignore. That would be a runaway moment for Stuart that I would not be able to control.

Chapter Four

November continued to blow in wetter and colder, knocking the remaining leaves off the trees and altering my view out the back window to the woods. At least there were pines to give green color to the otherwise bleak landscape that I trudged through on my daily mid-afternoon walk up to Highfields to observe the changing scenery of the valley and Mount Greylock beyond. The former tenants of the house, Monty Davis and Christa Champion, had left for New York after Labor Day and no new occupants had moved in; the only human activity was from a solitary worker who raked leaves, picked up broken tree limbs and put the garden to bed for the winter, as people referred to it. Surely someone stopped in to check on the interior of the house, but not even Annie, who seemed to know everything before the rest of us, had that information. It was a solitary walk up and back down on the path through the woods that gave me exercise and a break in the long workday at John's office.

A gust of cold air accompanied my entrance, making the thin woman who sat in the doctor's waiting room clutch her handbag closer as if to fend it off.

"Mrs. Rockmore, how are you?" I asked. She was one of Miss Manley's regular tea group.

"Well, thank you." She seemed to realize that was a silly answer for someone waiting in a doctor's office and qualified her answer, "I've been better."

Before I could tell her that the doctor would be with her shortly, he opened the door to his study and ushered her into the exam room. I took off my coat and anticipated his call for assistance but the look on Mrs. Rockmore's face told me that she didn't think he needed my help. John raised his eyebrows at me and I frowned, finding her attitude off-putting. I always took great care not to talk to anyone about the patients who came into the doctor's office, including Miss Manley or Glenda, and certainly not why they were there. In a big city hospital, you might gossip to the other nurses about a patient, or even to your family or close friends, but in a small town like West Adams, it would be a terrible breach of confidence. The absurd thing was that everyone seemed to know who came and went from his office anyway, what medicines were dispensed from the pharmacy, and the patients themselves often shared their maladies with their friends. Despite all this transparency among the townspeople, I knew we were held to a higher standard, and I was careful to maintain it. Still, I wondered what Mrs. Rockmore's problem was and would either hear about it from John himself or read it in the notes of her file.

I sat down to open the afternoon mail and saw an unusually large envelope addressed to Doctor John Taylor and Miss Agnes Burns. I chuckled knowing who it was from and wondered if she would persist in renaming me or if it were some game of hers. The envelope contained a cream-colored invitation elegantly executed by hand in calligraphy announcing the "Ersatz Christmas Celebration" at Browne's Castle for the weekend in December Hextilda had mentioned. I paused a moment, not certain of her intentions. Did she mean she planned to have an actual Christmas celebration but not on the traditional date? Or was it to be a substitute holiday in some other sense—such as *not* Christmas?

Enclosed were directions to her home, which were unnecessary; a list of suggested wardrobe to bring: two changes of formal dress, sweaters, wool slacks and warm boots, presumably not worn at the same time; and ice skates, which most young people possessed. A note at the bottom of that page was that cross-country skis and snow-shoes were available unless we had them already. Another sheet of paper had a schedule of events: Friday: Welcome cocktails, dinner, after-dinner games. Games? Were we going to play hide-and-seek in the castle? Sardines? Now, that would be fun in a huge house. Saturday: Breakfast, outdoor activities (the skating, skiing, or snowshoeing, I guessed), Lunch, Afternoon free, Evening cocktails, Christmas dinner, games. Sunday, much the same as Saturday. Farewell dinner. I guessed this meant that we were supposed to leave the next morning. I smiled at the juxtaposition of formality and absurdity that this pile of papers presented. There was, of course, a small RSVP card and envelope enclosed.

Mrs. Rockmore's exam may not have been lengthy, but judging from the murmuring behind the closed door, the discussion was considerable. She was a woman I had met several times at Miss Manley's, and I didn't find her welcoming or generous, but I still hoped she didn't have any serious issue. She came out and avoided eye contact with me but nodded her head in my direction. What was that about?

I plowed through the rest of the mail, aware that John had not seen what was sent, so I shared the extraordinary contents of the envelope. His eyebrows shot up and he shook his head but then laughed at the absurd weekend Hextilda had planned.

"I imagine it might be chilly to snowshoe in formal wear, but we'll see." He handed the papers back to me. "It's a good thing I still have a dinner jacket that fits."

"You men have it so easy. You can wear the same thing every night and nobody notices. Women have to bring a change of dress, shoes to match, complimentary jewelry...."

26

"You may not think I notice, but you have two perfectly good long dresses that would be appropriate."

"John. Those were summer dresses. Short sleeves, light colors. I need something entirely different for winter. I have some things at home in Pelham. I'll show you when we're there for Thanksgiving and you can tell me if they'll work."

He looked askance at me. "I don't know anything about what women should wear. Have your mother take you shopping."

I sighed. "Glenda will be in New York so perhaps I'll ask her. She loves shopping."

The door opened and Nina Lewis, the reverend's wife, poked her head around the corner and surveyed the empty room.

"Is now a good time?" she asked.

"Certainly," John said, preparing to go into the exam room.

"Things have been so quiet around here with Roger off to school and not the usual scrum of young men," Nina said.

"Did you know that Glenda's tenant, Douglas, is moving on, too?"

"Oh dear, she will miss the rent money."

"After all his trouble this past summer, he came over and told Miss Manley that he got an offer to direct an off-Broadway play. He is so anxious to start, he agreed to pay the next month's rent even though he won't be here."

"Do you think Cash Ridley had anything to do with it?"

"I don't know, but what a positive change for the poor man."

"Ready?" John asked Nina.

They were in there about a half hour, chatting most of the time and then it was quiet. John came out, went to his office, sorted through some files and pulled out a paper that he carried back, unknowingly allowing me to see it was some kind of dietary guide.

A few minutes later they emerged and the smile on her face and the welling in her eyes told me she was pregnant, although I didn't dare say anything.

"Sometime next week, perhaps you could help me with some

wardrobe issues," I said, and she nodded, too overcome with emotion to speak before she left.

John shook his head in exasperation at me. "I don't know why you are so concerned about our weekend. We're not going to be presented to royalty."

"You may not think so, but Hextilda may have other ideas."

* * *

John let his patients know that he would be gone for Thanksgiving, and we left early on Wednesday morning, bringing Miss Manley with us to Pelham to meet my parents, and then into Manhattan to Stuart and Glenda's for dinner. She sat in the front seat marveling at the many changes since her last trip south several years ago but also commenting on how sorry some of the roadside businesses looked due to lack of commerce. The Depression had hit everyone financially, whether they lived in a city or a town, but the countryside suffered more than other regions. Still, the weather-beaten billboards displayed the incongruous excitement of buying a new car—as if anyone could afford a new vehicle.

I began to smile when I saw the high granite hills looming over the roadway as we went south of farm country and saw a sign for Bear Mountain. I leaned forward from the back seat. "We used to come up here on the weekend to hike and picnic."

"It's a beautiful area," Miss Manley commented.

"Farther south there is another large park with reservoirs, natural lakes, waterfalls and hiking paths."

"Did you even camp out?" John asked.

"No. My mother was concerned about my father's health from the Great War's gas damage. She thought sleeping out in the damp was not a good idea. But I think the thought of bears prowling around might have been a strong reason, too."

Miss Manley turned a startled face toward me. "Are there bears in Pelham?"

I felt like laughing but instead turned deadly serious. "You'll see."

Directly ahead was the entrance to the Bear Mountain Bridge that would take us over the Hudson to Westchester County as we drove through the increasingly suburban towns north of New York City.

"I've never come this way to New York," Miss Manley said. "I've traveled by train and bus and the only times by car we stayed on the other side of the Hudson. I had no idea this area was so populated. Bears, indeed."

It was probably a strange thing for her to see what looked like contiguous habitation when we passed through many towns and villages as we drove south and then east through Bronxville and Mount Vernon and finally approached Pelham.

Home.

Everything was so familiar and yet somehow smaller than I had remembered and a bit sad looking now that the leaves were gone from the trees. When I was here last, it was the beginning of summer and I thought I would be working in one of the City's big hospitals where I trained before Glenda told me of the opportunity of assisting a country doctor for a short period of time. That part-time, short period had now stretched to five months, yet it seemed like years.

It was wonderful to see my parents again and they were thrilled to see that Miss Manley was indeed an elderly woman, a perfect chaperone in their eyes. As we sat for tea, I could see they were a bit more hesitant on how to evaluate John, who they had assumed might be an older person, perhaps married with children. I suddenly realized how much I had kept from them; not just the lurid events of the past summer, but the small detail that I worked with an attractive, single man who smiled at me with affection.

My mother gave me what we called the 'high sign,' a bit of an eyebrow lift, and then asked me to help her bring out some of the refreshments. Once we got to the kitchen, she tried her hardest to refrain from peppering me with questions; that lasted as long as it took to get the cream out of the refrigerator.

"My heavens, but Doctor Taylor is a very good-looking man," she said.

"Yes," I answered calmly.

"Well?"

"Well, what?"

My mother took me by the shoulders and looked me in the eye, which took some doing since I am much taller than she. It had the effect and I blushed.

"I thought so!"

"Everything has been on the up and up, Mother." I only called her Mother when I wanted to be stern.

"I hope so. And I would like it to stay that way. You're still a young woman." She pottered about putting the cream into a small pitcher. "And he'll be staying in your brother's room while he's here. At the other end of the hall."

"Of course," I said in the most convincing tone I could muster. I took the plate of cookies through into the parlor.

Tea was a brief affair, as we had promised to take Miss Manley to Manhattan so she could have dinner with Stuart and Glenda. We drove south past the cars streaming north toward the end of the workday as the sun went down. I had positioned myself in the front seat to give directions to their apartment on the East Side.

"Good God, this traffic is horrible," John said, pushing his hat back on his head. Do people live like this every day?"

"The saner folks take a bus or subway since it's faster. Walking is sometimes the quickest method of travel."

We pulled in front of the apartment building and John managed to have the doorman let us park for a few minutes while we made the transfer. Stuart's place was on the fifth floor and luckily there was an elevator to take us there. We didn't stay long as Stuart greeted us, took Miss Manley's suitcase off down a short hall while Glenda asked us to sit for a moment. We explained about the car out front, which made her eyes light up.

"A car! Let's go to Chinatown for dinner!"

I knew she didn't like cooking and I didn't smell anything in progress, so it seemed a good idea, although I wondered how their future child would fare without nourishment beyond milk, formula or delicatessen food. After freshening up, Miss Manley, hat still on her head, was whisked out and onto a wild ride downtown for perhaps the first Chinese meal of her life.

It was a raucous place that Stuart said was entirely authentic, meaning he could not communicate with the waiter and had no idea what to order. But the place was busy, and he made the hackneyed comment that, because Chinese people were eating there, it must be good. The menu was huge and, of course, we chose the most familiar and probably boring entrees although it came to the table quickly and hot. After a long day's drive, we were happy to put an early end to the evening and drive back to Pelham, with my promise to Glenda that she should help me select some clothing for my December weekend.

I didn't realize how tired I was, but I could not doze off since John didn't know the way back to Pelham, which seemed endless but was, in reality, not that far. True to form, my parents were still up waiting in the living room, listening to the radio, my father reading the newspaper and my mother doing needlepoint. He ceremoniously ushered John to my brother's room, which had two single beds, showed him the bathroom, asked if he needed anything and then made himself scarce.

My room was at the other end of the hall, and John and I had that awkward moment of meeting in the hall en route to and from the bathroom.

"Your parents are lovely," he said, smiling and hugging me. "And so are you."

Chapter Five

My brother Eddie burst into the house just before noon on Thanksgiving, having grabbed a ride from a classmate, and was full of excitement at being home. Suitcase dumped on the ground, hugs and kisses all around, he was stopped short by the sight of John, perhaps thinking that the doctor was going to be some white-haired relic invited out of pity.

Eddie caught my eye, smiled and then shook John's hand vigorously.

"Well, when's dinner? It smells great. I'm starved," he said.

"You're always starved," I commented, and he gave me another hug.

"I missed your teasing."

It was my mother's usual simple yet satisfying feast that left us groggy by late afternoon. John and Eddie played a game of chess, I napped next to my mother on the sofa, and we passed a quiet evening, having saved the pies for dinner.

The next day, I was due to meet Glenda in the City so we could shop for evening clothes for me. Stuart was taking his aunt to see some sights and my father and John went on an improvised tour of

Revolutionary War sites in the area. The house was bustling as we went our separate ways, with Eddie still fully asleep in the bedroom he had shared with John the night before.

Lord &Taylor was my destination with a roll of money in my handbag and another sewn into the pocket of my coat—my mother's precautions. She once told me that people used to put money in their shoes in the event they got robbed and I always wondered if folks still did that. Grand Central Station still looked as glamorous as ever. We met under the big clock, then arm and arm walked to our favorite department store just blocks away. There were no idlers along the streets here as every shop owner shooed shabby looking men away from their storefronts and policemen scowled at anyone they thought shouldn't be there. It was strange to know that this part of the City at this time of day was reserved for the well to do, and the folks hardest hit had to stay somewhere else, like the Bowery or neighborhoods with which I wasn't even familiar.

Those disturbing thoughts left my head the moment the doors of Lord &Taylor opened, and we caught the intoxicating scent of perfume from the ground floor counters. But we were on a mission and made for the elevators up to the floors where formal wear was displayed. We had decided that the red velvet dress with white satin trim at the three-quarter length sleeves that I wore to the Christmas formal last year would be just the right thing for a Christmas, ersatz or not. Was that only last year? I could hardly remember my date's name, much less anything interesting about the evening except that my fellow nursing classmates were there.

The selection of dresses was extensive, but it seemed the designers assumed we all lived in well-heated rooms; the majority of the garments were silk, many of them sleeveless, some of them cut low in the back—more like something a Hollywood actress would wear. Luckily, an older saleswoman sensed our dismay and steered us toward an alcove that had clothing with more coverage. I fell in love with a dark blue velvet dress with a sweetheart neckline and long puffed sleeves; strangely the length was fine although it needed taking in around the torso.

I emerged from the dressing room tugging at the extra fabric and Glenda stood from the upholstered chair in which she had been sitting.

"That's the one. Stop yanking at the fabric."

"We'd be happy to do the alterations in-house," the saleswoman said.

"I'm afraid I live out of town, and I need it relatively soon. I think I know someone who can alter it."

She smiled and fussed around with the hem while Glenda looked at the price tag.

"Not bad," she whispered. Then louder, "Do you think the emerald tiara will be a bit too much with it?"

The saleslady was not fooled a bit and smiled at our fantasy.

My mother loved my choice of dress and offered some jewelry to enhance it—alas, not a tiara—and we chatted as I took winter clothing down from the attic and packed it into suitcases.

"Tell me about this weekend event," she said.

"This woman is an eccentric author and lives in what can only be described as a castle, in a valley in southern Vermont."

My mother stopped what she was doing and stared at me.

"Really. She lives alone—well, not entirely alone—and I suppose has invited us for company."

"That is the strangest thing I ever heard. What is her name?"

I told her and she looked surprised.

"She writes *those* novels."

"Yes. Have you read any of them?"

"Margaret Fulton has read many of them and lent me one. It was quite racy." Her face got pink, and I laughed.

"That's wonderful! Based on your description, you might think she was some tempestuous vixen, while in reality she is a dotty older woman with a strange sense of humor."

My mother sat on the bed with that wrinkle of worry between her eyes. "Are you sure it is safe to go there?"

"Of course. John will be with me."

"And the sleeping arrangements?" she said more tartly.

"Naturally, I haven't asked, but she knows we're not married."

My mother stood up and said, "Just be certain about that."

The conversation was over.

Eddie had wandered off with his high school friends for the day while John and my father stayed out until it was dark. We had a Thanksgiving repeat dinner for which my mother apologized as if we were the only family in the world who ate leftovers. Midway through the evening of listening to the radio, the phone rang, and Stuart told us that Miss Manley was feeling poorly, that he would bring her over in the morning so that we could take her back to West Adams on Saturday. That spoiled whatever plans we may have had for the next day and cut our visit short but needs must, as my mother always says.

Stuart and his flashy Packard, which he had to keep in a garage somewhere in the City for fear of theft, vandalism or parking tickets, pulled up early on Saturday morning and the two grim-faced relatives trooped into the house. John and I exchanged a look, telegraphing our understanding that it was not a physical ailment that troubled Miss Manley but something else.

Stuart refused refreshment of any kind, gave his aunt a peck on the cheek and abruptly left. There was an awkward moment before John asked if she was feeling all right and she made a sour face.

"I will be soon enough, I think." She declined to sit and because she stood waiting, we hustled to get our luggage downstairs.

"We'll get you back home early," I said stupidly.

My parents were sorry to see us go so soon, and I had to ask them to say goodbye to Eddie, still asleep from a late night out with friends, and we escorted the stony-faced Miss Manley to the back seat and made our way back to West Adams with minimal conversation. It wasn't until several weeks later that we got the full story, but first there were the preparations for our weekend with Mrs. Browne.

John teased me mercilessly when I asked whether we should bring a hostess gift or an actual Christmas gift and what it should be. He always had a facetious answer, which annoyed my sense of trying to do the proper thing. I was curious to know if we were the only guests but knew that it was impolite to ask. His response was, "Why not ask?" and he began to pick up the telephone before I yelped and asked him not to call.

I made an inventory of what clothing, accessories and toiletries I should bring according to the schedule that we had been sent but hid it as he came into the room, pretending it was a list of intended Christmas presents. Then he teased me about what I was going to get him for a holiday gift, and I told him a stocking full of coal would be just the thing. I think he knew I was preoccupied with facing an unknown and possibly intimidating social situation and his teasing was meant to calm my nerves, but it only made them worse.

Out of his sight back in my room, I sorted through the winter clothes I had brought from home and decided to air out the mothball-smelling sweaters, checking to make sure that none had holes or stains. I don't know why I cared so much about making an impression on Mrs. Browne or not making a terrible faux pas, and finally the day before we were to leave, I woke up and decided that I didn't care a whit for Hextilda or her silly affectations or however much money she had. I was Agnes Burnside—not Burns—and I was proud of it.

There.

I was over the anxiety at last.

Almost.

John had got a doctor in Pittsfield to cover for him over the weekend, and with all the office tasks completed in both Adams and West Adams, there was that wonderful sense of relief of leaving obligations behind and adventure ahead. The car was packed with more suitcases than any reasonable person would bring because of the changes of clothes needed for various activities and having to pack my evening dresses loosely with tissue paper to minimize wrinkles.

"I once read an article about an English country weekend in a magazine and what surprised me was the physical activities during the day coupled with the fancy dress at night. Do you think that's what it will be like?" I was trying to sound calm, but my nervousness was getting the better of me. "Fox hunting and so on?"

John looked over at me. "Can you ride a horse?"

"Not well," I admitted.

"I don't imagine there will be fox hunting. Although I didn't take a thorough look at the property, I didn't see anything like stables."

"That's good. I don't think I would like it." I hoped I wasn't going to do something gauche in front of her.

We made the first turn-off and felt it was considerably colder this trip; we could hear the crunch of frozen leaves under the tires as we progressed through the dark forest. I rolled down the window to see if we were the only car to come through, and it certainly seemed that was the case if this was the only way in and out. It would be almost impossible to find your way at night as there were no landmarks, just endless stands of pines and the narrow, one-car pathway. Then, as before, the road widened considerably, and we were perched at the top of the rise that allowed us to look down at the castle below.

"Homey, isn't it?" John asked.

"I can't imagine a more comfortable place to spend a cold December weekend," I replied. *She must have heat in the house,* I thought.

Our first steps inside the entry told me that Hextilda was not one to skimp on comfort as the interior temperature, though chilly, was warm enough for me in my wool skirt, tights and a thick sweater. Eleanor had opened the door to us, said Bruce would bring our luggage upstairs, and asked if we would like to see our rooms.

We followed her through the impressive Great Room, where an enormous balsam fir stood in the corner, emitting its pungent scent, then through an archway to a hall and up a long staircase that took us to the balcony that went around three sides of the room below. A blaze was going in the fireplace and the woodsmoke infused this upper gallery, bringing back memories of summer camp and roasting frankfurters on long forks.

"Here is your room, sir," Eleanor said, opening a door close to the top of the stairs. I peeked around her shoulder and saw twin beds and a small wall-hung shaving sink in the far corner. "The lavatory is down the hall." I almost giggled because one of our high school teachers always used that old-fashioned term instead of washroom or bathroom.

John stood still a moment wondering if he should follow us, gave a shrug and did so. We passed more doors, then she pointed to the closed bathroom door, then turned the corner and we came to what would be my room. It, too, had twin beds but was larger and I thought more pleasantly decorated than what was probably the bachelor guest room.

"Mrs. Browne is still working. She said you're free to entertain yourself until she is done in about an hour. If you don't need anything else just now." She left us there and John stepped into my room, being careful to leave the door open.

"Oh, sure, you get the best room," he said enfolding me in a hug.

"Of course. But then we don't know what the family's bedrooms are like."

A little self-conscious about our embrace with Eleanor just down the hall and Bruce likely on the way up, I broke away to walk to the window with the pretext of admiring the view. "Isn't this fantastic?" I said. "Why don't we go for a walk?"

"That's fine. I'll just help Bruce with the bags and get my walking boots on."

I guessed this was the usual female guests' room as it was decorated with floral chintz curtains although, on closer inspection, I found them lined with a heavy flannel. Yes, it was going to be cold in here tonight with that large single-glazed window. Some thumping and bumping noises from the hall told me that Bruce, large as he was,

was wrestling with the number of suitcases we had brought. First, he deposited John's, then mine, without a word even after I thanked him. I fished around in the larger case and took out heavy boots, then thought to take out the formal dresses and hang them up to relax before dinner, hours away. I was curious to know what the rest of the property looked like before we lost the sun for the day.

What an extraordinary property it was, with no trees in the immediate perimeter of the structure, just as you see in photos of actual European castles. As we walked away from the building, we turned to get a better look of its situation in the valley.

"Now, a real castle would never be positioned in such a vulnerable spot," John said. "If the valley were narrower, the enemy could rain arrows down at you from all angles and at a more advantageous height." He swept his arm out to show me.

"But surely arrows can't travel that far? I'm still rooting for a moat."

"Those stinking things? Where do you think they dumped all the chamber pots?"

"Ugh. Really? Okay, no moat then. But you must admit the castle is charming. And there are no invaders likely."

"And likely cost old man Browne an arm and a leg to purchase, take apart, ship and reassemble."

"I wonder if any of her family is interested in living here permanently?"

John shrugged his shoulders. "It has got to be a beast to heat and maintain."

We continued across the open ground almost a half-mile in one direction before we could feel an incline in elevation, but it was gradual as we continued. The sun was gone behind the mountains but had not yet set, and it would be colder still in a short while.

"Have you had enough exercise?" John asked me.

"Yes, let's go back. We can explore in the other direction tomorrow if time permits."

Leaves had blown in across the otherwise barren ground and they crunched beneath our booted feet. Looking up I saw a car in the distance coming down the same long drive that we had descended earlier, and I pointed.

"That looks like Fred's car," John said, smiling.

I hoped so as the notion of spending an entire weekend as the sole guests still seemed a bit strange to me. We quickened our steps so that by the time we reached the front of the house the horn was honked at us, and Fred waved from the car's open window.

John trotted up to the car and they shook hands and pounded each other on the back.

"Delighted to see you!" Fred said. "And Mother didn't tell me you were coming."

"She didn't tell us either," I added.

"Like a true fiction author, she likes to keep everybody in suspense."

Chapter Six

Fred took a small suitcase out of the trunk of his car and John teased him, "You pack light! Don't you know we're supposed to do dinner jackets and all that?"

"Of course, old man. I know the drill. But I've got all that stuff here. With my schedule in Boston, do you think I have time for fancy dress?"

They chuckled at each other, and it was good to see John relaxed and enjoying his old friend. Fred dumped his suitcase in the entry and beckoned us to follow him as he led us through an archway toward what he called the sitting room.

"So much more comfortable than the Great Room," he said sarcastically. "Sometimes, I don't know what my father could have been thinking."

The sitting room was as relaxed as the other was imposing and had several low couches upholstered in a green fabric, end tables and armchairs; it was perfect for a cozy chat. Fred reached over to a small table near the door and asked if we wanted sherry, which was exactly the thing after a walk in the cold air.

"I'd ask Eleanor for tea, but she is up to her eyeballs in some colossal dinner my mother has planned." He brought the small glasses over to where we sat.

"I'm sorry she has to go to all this trouble by herself," I said.

"Don't worry, she's enlisted two young women from Stamford to assist. But I still like to keep out of her way," he said, feigning fright. He took a glass for himself, proposed a toast, "Here's to the only sane people in this house." He knocked his down in one gulp, his prominent Adam's apple bobbing as he swallowed. Where his mother had a round, cheerful face, Fred's was all angles, high cheekbones and sharp chin. But it was a pleasant face, nonetheless.

"If I could ask, how did your father come to find the buildings that he transported here? Did he travel quite a bit?"

"Yes, for his widespread business interests. But it was my mother who pulled him into the Scottish heritage thing."

"Fred, I'm sorry, we haven't had a chance to say hello to your mother yet," John said.

He looked at his wristwatch. "She'll still be dictating to Adele. The secretary. I guess you haven't met her yet. Mother has a strict schedule for herself, and she'll be reclined on a chaise longue in her study rattling off those blustery romances of Scotland to Adele's speedy shorthand."

It was an amusing picture he painted of his mother and although teasing, he had great affection for her.

"Anyway, my mother's maiden name is Cumming, which is of the Comyn clan in the Scottish Highlands. Of course. They were pivotal when Robert the Bruce was trying to coalesce the various groups that then became hostile to one another and the Comyns lost out. There are the remains of their castle in Fort Williams and naturally not all of them were killed off, they just didn't have the same power base or clout as before. And like many other Scots, they have maintained centuries of animosity toward the MacGregor clan, the Campbells, and others."

"That's a long time to bear a grudge," I said.

"I've come to understand that maintaining a ferocious hate

toward an enemy can sometimes be an invigorating thing for people. John, do you remember those two old men who came into the hospital at the same time as the result of a car smashing into their chessboard at the park?"

"Oh, yes!"

"These two men would play chess every day, and you would think that was because they were best friends, but they couldn't stand one another."

"Insanely jealous rivals at the game," John started to laugh.

"They weren't badly injured by the crash—one had abrasions and a possible sprain and the other had twisted his leg as he fell—but the physical injuries were nothing compared to the insults they hurled at one another. Each one claimed the other had somehow cheated and then there was an argument about where the pieces should be when they resumed the game." Now Fred was laughing, too.

"The one with the bad leg claimed the other must have landed on his head, otherwise he would remember things correctly."

"It sounds like your hospital afforded some amusement, at least."

"The other patients in the admitting room, some of whom were quite ill, got fed up with the invective and suddenly there was shouting, and a fight almost broke out. All because of an interrupted chess match."

"And by that story you mean to let me know that grudges and rivalry can enliven someone's life?" I asked.

"In the case of the Comyns, lives were lost, property was forfeited, and rank took a tumble, so it was more than verbal abuse they suffered. Still, my mother's family has been in the States for more than one hundred and fifty years and you would think all that was behind them. When she started her writing career, it allowed her to revive the Comyn name, although well before her time it was spelled Cumming, and through her novels, elevate her family to where they should have been."

"That's quite lovely," I said to their astonished faces. "Wouldn't it be wonderful to have great-great-grandchildren write about you with awe and enthusiasm and have other people feel the same?"

Fred gave me a long hard look before he spoke. "Yes, it would be. As long as said person made sure I was handsome, dashing, fearless and the best doctor in Boston!"

"Here, here!" John said, holding up his near-empty glass and downing the rest.

I blushed at the attention but realized that in their minds they had stepped away from their everyday thoughts and projected themselves into the future and what their legacy would be. As active, dedicated doctors, they would leave a significant legacy, even if they didn't know what that might yet be.

"Good heavens! What is all the noise?" Hextilda stood in the doorway, pretending to glower at her son and the two of us. Fred stepped forward and kissed her on the cheek.

"You should have told me that you had invited John and Aggie," he scolded her.

"And ruin the surprise?" Her smile lit up her face, and a glimmer was in her eye.

"Who was your hero running from this week?" he asked her.

"Pour me a sherry, dear, and you shall hear all about it." She said and he poured, refilling our glasses as well.

"Cheers everyone," she said. "In some ways, my original method of writing longhand was superior in that when I wrote Alistair into a particularly difficult corner, I could go back some pages and scribble in whatever character or device that would help him get out of it. Since I've had Adele, her incredible speed makes me dictate faster than I could ever write down the words, but then good old Alistair is in a pickle once again and I have to stop, ask her to go back, and then I make a mental note to insert the lifesaver."

"He sounds like he has nine lives," John said.

"Per book," she laughed.

"I thought they were romance books," I said.

"Action *and* romance. I was aiming for the male and female audience but no matter how much action or how alluring the women who come into his life, it is the women who buy the preponderance of my books. All sixteen of them to date."

"That's an extraordinary body of work."

She laughed. "A little more than eighteen years of it, although I am getting weary of putting my poor dear Scot through the wringer yet again."

"We keep trying to get Mother to branch out into something that's not so exhausting."

"Such as?" John asked.

"She's been to Scotland so many times—right there is a travel book that practically writes itself," Fred said.

Hextilda took a sip of her sherry and made a slight sneer. "Frederick, I know you think that's a wonderful idea, but I can't do it sitting here. I would have to go back, revisit places I've been already, go to places I would rather not go..."

"What are those?" I asked.

"Glasgow, if you must know. A very rough city. It would be extremely difficult to extol the beauties of that gritty place."

"Come on, Mother, there are some beautiful parks, gardens and homes."

"Yes, aside from the Cathedral, Kibble Palace and the architecture, I would run out of positive things to say."

"You could concentrate on the Highlands," I suggested.

Hextilda looked at me with interest. "Of course! Why not? It limits the scope of the work considerably and if my publisher likes it and it sells well, I could expand to other areas. You are a clever girl!"

I blushed at her praise but had to agree that it was the most logical course of action for her. And it would support the sales of her fiction books.

John winked at me in appreciation.

Hextilda put her glass on a nearby table and stood up. "Time to put my feet up for a bit. Then cocktails at six, dinner at seven." She walked to the doorway.

"Any more surprises, Mother?"

"Oh, yes, plenty. You'll see."

I raised my eyebrows and looked at John, who shrugged.

"It's getting dark already," Fred said. "I think I'll freshen up and see what's hanging in my closet."

"Good idea," John said. "Aggie?"

"I need to start reading one of your mother's books," I said.

Fred laughed. "Funny you should mention that. There happens to be at least one in every room of the house." He went to a cabinet in the far corner, opened it and shuffled around inside. "Might as well start at the beginning," he said producing a thick volume titled *Romance in the Heather.*

"Phew. I'd better get started." And when the men left the room, I took off my boots, curled my feet up under me and began to read. Like Stuart's book, at least the one I had tried to read but gave up on, it got off to a roaring start. But unlike his, she had long descriptive passages about the countryside, the scents of the plants, the sounds of the wildlife and birds that made it much more engrossing. Her characters came to life instantly and vibrantly with their desires and emotions on display so that you got a glimpse of where the conflicts were going to occur later on in the narrative. It wasn't just an action-adventure book; it touched on the reader's deep feelings as it propelled the story forward. And yes, the heaving bosom of the heroine and the smoldering eyes of Alistair made for a steamy book.

I had just begun the third chapter when I felt eyes upon me and saw a young girl standing in the doorway, looking curiously at me.

"Miss?"

"Hello," I said, not having a clue who she was.

"I'm Mariah. I'm helping out for the weekend. Mrs. Mowbray asked if there was anything you needed before the cocktail hour."

I looked at my watch and saw that it was five-thirty and almost leaped out of the chair.

"Thank you, I'd better get ready." I put my boots back on and looked up to see that she had gone. The book and I went upstairs to get ready for the next episode of the weekend at the Castle.

Chapter Seven

lthough my room had a tiny sink in the corner, I took my wash bag and looked for more extensive accommodations in the lavatory down the hall. The door I came to was closed, I knocked and heard someone answer from behind what turned out to be the locked door. Now what?

Fred, in a dinner jacket, had just exited a room on the opposite side of the gallery that stretched around three walls of the upper story and seeing my dismay came to the rescue. In a house this large, of course there were more bathrooms, I just didn't know where they were, so he directed me to one several doors down.

I don't think I had ever seen such a huge bathroom in my life. It was as large as my bedroom here, with tiny white and black tiles making designs on the floor, a massive clawfoot tub and a sink that you could bathe a baby in while a separate small room held the toilet. There was a pile of fluffy white towels on a long bench, although I had brought one of the towels provided in my room. There wasn't time now but tomorrow I would find an excuse to take a long, hot soak in the tub after placing a Do Not Disturb sign on the door.

Back in my room, I was pleased to find my formal dresses had eased out of their wrinkles and was surprised to find that while I had been reading downstairs, someone had unpacked the rest of my suit-cases. Hairbrush, comb and hand mirror were on the vanity top, my underclothes in the chest of drawers, everything very orderly. I thought I would wear the red dress tonight, keeping the fancier one for tomorrow evening, and I was glad it had long sleeves since the house was starting to feel chilly although the steam radiator along the wall was keeping up a gentle warmth. A pearl necklace, a glittery clip in my hair, a touch of powder and lipstick and Aggie, the quick-change artist, as I was known in nursing school, was ready for cock-tails. From the clinking of glassware that I heard as I exited the room, it seemed our cocktail hour would be in the Great Room in front of the massive fire. I looked over the gallery rail and saw that Fred and John were already downstairs, glass in hand and deep in conversa-tion. All hopes of a dramatic entrance down a grand staircase were dashed by there being two sets of stairs, both of them leading to the hallways that flanked the largest room in the Castle. As I approached the two men, I saw a small plate of hors d'oeuvres set on a nearby table, which reminded me that I was very hungry.

Fred offered me a drink of whiskey, and the young girl who had seen me in the sitting room earlier appeared with a tray of small bits of diced meat on miniature toasted squares.

"That looks delicious," I said, taking one and thought it was a strange texture, some kind of odd-tasting chopped liver, but not off-putting.

"Aye, a true Scot!" Fred exclaimed.

I look perplexed.

"You've just had your taste of real haggis," he explained. The two men toasted me with a sip of whiskey.

"It was rather...interesting," I said.

"That is Mother's first initiation rite to anyone who comes to Browne's Castle for the first time. That, and the exquisite whiskey."

"Here's to your mother's excellent taste," I said, raising my glass.

"I'm glad someone appreciates it," Hextilda said, making an

entrance in an elaborate gown with a plaid skirt that I assumed had some clan significance. She wore a ruffled, low-cut blouse that showed off a spectacular necklace of what had to be real gems and a sprig of heather on her left shoulder. Very festive, very Scottish and very expensive.

"Pour me a tot, darling Frederick," she said, holding her face up for a kiss on the cheek from him.

"Thank you so much for inviting us," John said.

"It will be fun, I can assure you. But only if you dare to participate in all the fun and games and get out at least once a day for some exercise."

"I was looking forward to wearing the snowshoes, but it looks like the weather is not cooperating," I said.

"Don't be so sure. It can change in a matter of minutes," she said.

"Everything can change in a matter of minutes," Fred said.

We all looked at him in surprise and he smiled a bit. "Sorry, that sounded very portentous."

"Did you mean *pretentious?*" John winked at me.

"Do you remember that one patient we worked on as residents in med school?"

John nodded.

"Oh, Frederick. Don't go on about those morbid hospital stories. Pass me some haggis, dear," she said to me, sitting down heavily in an ornate chair. I obliged but I wanted to hear the story.

"Some other time, then."

We were quiet for a few moments until Hextilda started on an entirely different topic. "I may have finished with my Scots hero for now."

"Really, Mother?" Fred could hardly suppress a smile.

"There is probably some other intriguing nationality that I could use. Can't you think of some group of people who used to be admired and are now in a difficult state—and they go through hardships, et cetera, et cetera?" She put her hand to her chin in thought.

"The American working man?" John suggested.

"Don't be boring. There's nothing glamorous about men selling pencils on the street corner. I meant dashing, inspiring, stylish..."

"The American doctor?" Fred suggested, hiding his face by taking another sip of whiskey.

"What do you think, Miss Burns?"

"Burnside," I corrected her, but she waved her hand at me as if I had been in error.

"I really couldn't say. I've only just started reading your first book and it is very absorbing."

"Absorbing? I should think so. You can't imagine how many rewrites I had to do to make it that way to satisfy my publisher. Anyway," she looked down at a delicate wristwatch, "we can always discuss this further during dinner."

The young girl appeared at the archway and signaled to Fred. He went over to her, talked a moment and then he waved his hand to John and all three talked briefly before leaving.

"Well!" Hextilda said, clearly annoyed that most of her audience had made a hasty exit.

I was intimidated by her conversational style of hopping from one topic to another and dreaded having to hold up my end until the men got back. Luckily, there was a commotion from the front entryway that drew our attention, a crashing and scraping that made Hextilda smile.

"Well, they're here at last."

Into the room came an unhappy-looking couple, one a taller, stouter version of Fred and a small woman with dark hair barely visible under a cloche hat, a scowl on her face.

"Allan, darling," Hextilda said, holding her hand out. He came forward frowning, leaned over and kissed her on the cheek. "And the ever-cheerful Joan," she continued.

"Hello, Mother," the woman said, not approaching. She looked over at me.

"I'm Aggie Burnside," I said, standing and offering my hand for a greeting that was received none too graciously. Allan shook my hand perfunctorily and began to take off his overcoat. He wore a pinstriped business suit, and his wife was also dressed in day wear, which clearly did not please his mother.

"Darling, not here. Go on up and change for dinner. Chop, chop!"

"Where the devil is Bruce? I had to drag the bags in myself."

The young girl appeared again at the archway and made her way into the Great Room, putting Allan's overcoat over her arm. "I'll do it, Miss. Bruce got a cut in the kitchen and the doctors are sewing it up."

"Two of them? Well, I suppose it will go more quickly that way. I hope there is no gore on the roast!" Hextilda laughed at her own joke. "Dinner is in a half hour," she said in the direction of her son and his wife.

I really wanted to check on the progress of the operation in the kitchen but realized three would be more than a crowd and it would be impolite to leave my hostess by herself, so I sat again and sipped my whiskey. The petulant pair left the room and appeared up in the gallery a few minutes later, engaged in a hushed argument.

"Charming, isn't she?"

I didn't know what to say.

"They've been married a long time, probably longer than either of them wanted, but that's life." She glanced up at them disappearing into one of the rooms at the far end of the gallery where Fred's room was.

"Do they have any children?" I asked for something to say.

"Yes. Two beautiful and utterly spoiled girls. They are off at school, thank goodness, or we should have to put up with them whining about nothing to do. So, tell me about yourself," she said, turning the force of her personality on me.

What could I possibly say that would be of interest to her? I have had a most ordinary life so far. Except for the murders in West Adams, that is. But I wasn't going to talk about that. I was desperately trying to think of something interesting to say and she was becoming impatient.

"John said you are a nurse. Have you ever seen a childbirth?"

I raised my eyebrows at that and nodded.

"I've experienced it, of course," she said. "Three times, but I've never seen a baby being born."

There was some noise at the front entry as the young girl struggled with three suitcases into the Great Room, through an archway and thumped up the stairs with them. She reappeared at the near end of the gallery, breathing heavily before making the long walk around to where Allan and Joan's room was.

"Well?"

"What was it you wanted to know?" I asked.

"My heroine is 'with child,' as they say and has been chased around the Highlands for a few chapters now, her dear Alistair overcome with his own troubles and tormented by the English officers who have loathed him since the first book. Oh, I hope I haven't given anything away," she said with a smile. Of course, she hadn't. It was obvious that was the main conflict in the book: the Scots versus the English and the love of Alistair and Gwendolyn amid the strife.

"As a result of running hither and yon, our dear heroine goes into labor. Now, I am wrestling with how to depict the event. It needs to be realistic but not too graphic. That seems ridiculous considering most of my readers are women and most of them have given birth. Nonetheless, I don't want them skipping ahead or putting the book down altogether."

"Who is with her?" I asked.

"Well, no one," Hextilda said as if it were obvious.

"She is going to give birth out in the wilds of Scotland by herself? Is the baby expected to live?"

She stared at me for a long moment. "Oh, no, you have just ruined everything! You're right, she can't just pop the baby out by herself, pick it up and go on her merry way. I suppose women have done it in the past, but a modern woman couldn't imagine it. Blast you! Now I'll have to invent a secondary character who is running away with her!"

I was silent while I saw her brow furrow in thought. "I think I have it. She has escaped with the daughter of the local midwife who, of course, has picked up all rudimentary knowledge when assisting her mother. But then again, she doesn't know all that she needs to know. Hmmm. The baby could be in the breech position, which would add to the urgency of the situation. They find shelter somewhere, maybe one of those little huts where the shepherds spend the night, but there is no fire, no boiling water, no clean linen. Oh, that's a wonderful idea, Aggie! Perhaps I should call the character Agnes, as I assume that is your real name?"

I was flabbergasted at how quick her mind worked and how in a matter of minutes someone sprang to life with an entire history and was faced with so many hurdles.

"Yes, it is Agnes. And if you want the character to look like me, I shouldn't mind at all."

"Good idea. We'll have to give you long hair, of course. And maybe not so tall."

* * *

By the end of a half hour, John and Fred had returned to the Great Room and the look John gave me confirmed it was not that serious a surgery. A few minutes later, Allan and Joan appeared to Fred's astonishment.

"Well, old man, I didn't know you were going to be here!" He shook his brother's hand and that of his sister-in-law, who had changed from her street clothes to a long olive-green dress with a slight train in the back.

"Good God, Joan. Do you still have that hideous thing? It doesn't do your complexion any favors. Look at the bright frock that Aggie has. Just the thing, so festive, so happy," Hextilda said.

"What is there to be festive about? It's December, it's colder than death outside, so pitch dark that it's a wonder we didn't crash into a tree. What's so important about this weekend, anyway?" Joan had a sour expression which, combined with her drab dress, made for a dour impression.

"Since we can't ever seem to round everyone up for a warm family Christmas, I thought we could recreate something similar," Hextilda said.

Allan scoffed loudly. "How about a whiskey, Fred. Make it a double."

I looked at Joan, wondering why he hadn't offered her anything to drink and sensing my discomfort, Allan said one word. "Teetotaler."

I managed a smile but wondered if things could get any more uncomfortable. I was about to find out.

The front door crashed open to loud voices and banging suitcases. In walked a slim, haughty young woman with her strawberry blonde hair cut in a head hugging bob, a long-fitted coat with a thick fox collar and a small hat perched on the back of her head.

"Well, look who's here!" she said, peeling off her coat and tossing it toward one of the chairs as she faced Allan. "Why didn't you tell me you were going to be here? She took the drink from Allan's hand and had a large gulp and looked around the room. "A Christmas tree! With no ornaments, no presents underneath?"

"And hello to you, Caroline," Hextilda said, not getting up from her chair.

"Hello, Mother," she answered, delivering a peck on the cheek. "Fred." He also got a slight kiss. "Joan." Nothing. The women barely made eye contact.

More noise at the front entry and we all turned to see an extraordinarily handsome man with dark hair and eyes come into the room and nod his head in our direction.

"This is José Pérez de Guzmán. You've heard me speak of him," Caroline stated rather than asked. She picked up one of the haggis toasts, frowned at it and put it back on the plate.

He bowed more deeply, his hand across his midsection. "The pleasure is all mine, Mrs. Browne. Fellow guests." Although his choice of words and manner were flowery and exotic, his English was excellent.

"You're late," Hextilda said, looking at her watch.

"We got a bit of a delayed start from the City but as you can see, we are already dressed for dinner, so no harm done." She had on a sleeveless silk dress that was set off at each shoulder with a jeweled dress clip. Her effortless glamor made me think my pearls were dowdy, but they had been a graduation present from my grandmother, and I would continue to wear them with pride.

"Where is Bruce?" Caroline asked.

"Had a bit of an accident in the kitchen. Cut his hand," Fred said.

She and Allan gave each other a look, then turned away. There was more going on here than I could follow.

"José, take off your coat. Come have a drink," she said.

The young girl who always silently appeared in the archway was back and announced that dinner was served.

The Brownes all gulped the remains of their drinks and stood, allowing their mother to take the lead and she looked to John, who offered his arm to her. Allan did the same for me, Fred paired up with his sister, leaving José to bring in Joan and we made a solemn procession out of the Great Room, through an archway, across a hall and through double doors into the candlelit dining room. Nameplates were at each place, and after I took my seat, I had a chance to look at the astonishing décor of the room.

One wall consisted of racks of antlers from small toward the wainscoting of the walls to enormous near the ceiling. The animal that walked around with such a weight on its head must have been colossal. On the adjacent wall were mounted stuffed heads of wild beasts that were certainly not native to Scotland or the United States, leading me to think that the late Mr. Browne was a hunter of some energy, if not skill. In a corner, behind the chair at the head of the table stood a bear on its hind legs, its eight-foot presence looming over the room. If the scene weren't so imposing it would have been almost ludicrous. I looked over at John, whose eyes were as wide as mine as we took in the room, the elaborate candelabra that spanned the dining table and the complicated place setting of plates, cutlery and glasses. I thought it best to watch my hostess and follow her lead in the choice of utensils.

The young woman who had attended to us earlier was one of the servers, accompanied by another so similar in appearance that they may have been sisters. They poured white wine into each of our glasses except for Joan who shook her head as they approached. When all were served, Hextilda proposed a toast.

"To the first, but not the last, Ersatz Christmas at Browne's Castle."

Everyone raised a glass, with Allan looking perplexed at her statement.

"So, this is to be Christmas this year?" he asked.

"With all your business and social engagements in the City as well as whatever it is the girls get up to, I decided to have my own kind of holiday. We've got our tree, no need to drag all those ornaments down from the attic and drape tinsel that doesn't look a bit like snow from the boughs. We're going to have a feast, of course, starting with trout, not from Scotland obviously, but some well-stocked stream somewhere." She waved her hand impatiently, not knowing where the fish came from.

The two young women each came in with a platter of trout almandine and I took a very small portion, sensing that there were to be many more courses to come.

"Of what else does you Ersatz Christmas consist?" Caroline asked in a bored tone.

"There will be games," she paused to enjoy the reactions of those around the table. John, José and I were interested, Allan and Caroline expressed a joint sigh, and Joan and Fred had no reaction at all. "Interesting games. And one where you all can create a plot for a new fiction book."

"I thought you were done with all that, Mother," Allan said.

"How can you think that? I'm working on one of the books right now. If I weren't smack up against a deadline, Adele would have been able to join us."

"You're not working her to the bone again, are you?" Fred asked.

"She enjoys the work, I pay her well and give her an acknowledgment in every one of my books. And she gets to live here in this beautiful house much of the year and Boston in the dead of winter."

"I think we are in the dead of winter already, so why are you both still here?"

"Deadlines, dear. And I so wanted everyone to enjoy this strange new holiday I have invented. How do you like the trout?"

Each one of us muttered words of praise as it was delicate with just a hint of the wild.

"I do hope this new holiday will not involve haggis or any of those other horrid, tasteless foods the Scots like so much," Caroline said.

"Like oatmeal?" Fred said, laughing.

"I guess we won't be having scones, either," added Allan.

"Don't be so provincial, Caroline. We are having a standing beef rib roast so all you carnivores can boast about how stuffed you are after dinner." She nodded to the women, who removed the fish plates; then Bruce appeared, wearing the same flannel shirt and suspenders as if he had just been chopping wood, with a bandage on one hand. He was carrying an enormous platter with a rib roast so large that it may have come from a moose. He passed it by Hextilda for her perusal then put it on a sideboard under the arrangement of antlers that cast strange shadows on him. The two women returned with large bowls of side dishes that they held out to each diner in turn to take our portion. Judging from the selection of accompaniments, I wondered if there would be room on the plate for the meat or space left in my stomach by the end of the meal. While Bruce carved, Mariah brought a serving plate around and while there were entire ribs available, mercifully there were smaller portions cut as well.

I looked down at Bruce's mis-matched socks and must have had a puzzled look on my face because Hextilda noticed and whispered, "He's color blind."

"Are you working on a new book, Mrs. Browne?" José asked drawing attention away from my observation.

"Yes, and I'm almost finished and thinking of going in a new direction."

"The travel journals I suggested?" Fred asked.

"That is very tempting, don't you think, Allan?"

"Hmm?" He was too engrossed in maneuvering a rib from the platter to his plate. "You're going traveling?"

"No, dear. Fred suggested that I write about Scotland from a traveler's point of view."

"If you ask me, that sounds more wholesome than violent romance books," Joan said.

"It's a good thing I didn't ask you, Joan. That's why I asked your husband."

Everyone was quiet but not as surprised as I would have thought. Evidently the insults were not a new thing between the two women.

"I've thought it over and I decided that I'm going to write a murder mystery. And all of you will be in it.

Chapter Eight

This should have been the moment for us all to drop our cutlery on the china, which is what Hextilda expected with that wicked smirk on her face, but to her dismay, no one did. This spoke more to her family's long familiarity with her dramatic flourishes than the substance of what she had said. What surprised me more was that John and I had first gone to see her at Fred's urging because she said someone was trying to kill her. Was this ploy about a murder mystery some way to ferret out who among those present might be most likely to have those intentions?

"Tell us more, Mother," came Caroline's bored voice. She pushed her food around the plate rather than eating anything, which explained how she maintained such a slim figure.

"I haven't got the plot just yet, but after dinner I thought we could play a little game."

Someone emitted a sorry sigh.

"Not a game, exactly, but a round robin where you quickly respond to some questions and that will help me with plot and motivations."

"That sounds splendid, Mother. I assume that you will put us in your acknowledgments?" Caroline asked.

"The hell with thank you. If we help you write this, we will be co-authors, correct?" Allan suggested.

Hextilda laughed at the suggestion.

"Too complicated for my publisher to figure out the royalties. Besides, the plot always changes as I write, and one part of me would like not to decide who the perpetrator is until I get almost to the end."

"Very clever. And who will the victim be?"

"The person most deserving," she said, her eyes scanning us each in turn. Joan looked annoyed, José was a bit surprised, as were John and I, but her two sons and daughter kept eating or moving food around on the plate as if these provocative remarks were natural.

The main meal was completed, the plates removed, and Hextilda asked that the Dundee cake be brought in. I think Caroline groaned slightly at this pronouncement.

"I've never had it. What's in it?" I asked.

"And you, a Scot," Hextilda stated rather than asked before I could correct her. "It's our version of a fruit cake but not so dark or dense and decorated beautifully by Eleanor with Marcona almonds in that special design."

"Swords and axes?" Caroline asked.

"No, you remember, it's a starburst design. There is some silly story about Mary Queen of Scots, no heroine of mine, not liking glacéed cherries as decoration, hence the almonds."

"There's a good topic for a book. A biography of Mary Queen of Scots," José suggested.

Hextilda harumphed in reply.

"You know it is said that however a biographer chooses to approach his or her," here a nod to his hostess, "subject, the author is invariably drawn into the life so completely that the product is almost always positive. Judging from your reaction, Mrs. Browne, and your strength of character, you would be the least likely person to fall to the charms of the late Queen as so many of her time and ours have."

"Caroline told me that your father was in the diplomatic service, and I see the apple did not fall far from the tree," she said.

José nodded to her as if she were royalty bestowing a compliment.

"Ah, here's the cake!" she said as Eleanor brought it in and placed it in front of Hextilda along with a knife and a serving tool.

"I have to tell you that, although this is a traditional Christmas cake in Scotland, since this is my version of Christmas, there is, of course, a bit of a twist. Some of you may have heard of the New Orleans king cake that is served on what we would call Twelfth Night. That cake has a bean or a little figure of the Christ child baked in and whoever gets that special piece has good luck for the rest of the year. I, of course, thought the bean too mundane so we've got a *bébé* in ours."

"Mother, you have done some odd things in your life, but creating this Ersatz Christmas along with some pagan custom disguised with religious symbolism has got to top all," Caroline said.

"Ah—but what if *you* get the *bébé*?" she teased back.

"If I break my teeth on it, it could hardly be considered good luck. And I think I am pretty lucky already," she added, looking directly at José, who nodded gallantly in return.

"I would have to agree, for the same reason," he said.

The cake was cut, the pieces handed around and everyone put their forks into the cake, gingerly waiting to hit the figurine. It was impossible to see it since there were dried fruits and raisins within, just like a typical fruitcake and Joan poked the tines of her fork up and down in her piece to Hextilda's annoyance.

"Oh! I've got it!" she shouted, picking it out of the crumbs with her fingers.

"Well done," everyone clapped, and she smiled broadly, absurdly pleased with herself.

When the excitement died down, Hextilda added, "I forgot to mention that the good luck comes in the form of another child." She laughed loudly and was the only person to do so as Allan and Joan were not amused, John and I glanced at each other while the others looked down at their plates.

"*You* are a horrid woman," Joan declared.

Hextilda stared back at her daughter-in-law. "Yes, I am. Can't help it. Now hurry up and finish because we have a game to play—in the Game Room, of course. She stood up, leaving us gaping at one another and quickly consuming the dessert and coffee.

It was Fred who directed us to the Game Room, through an archway toward the front of the house next to the sitting room where I had been reading earlier. It was primarily designed for a billiard table but also had a round table and chairs that could accommodate a good-sized poker party. Hextilda was already seated and motioned us to sit wherever we wished. Once positioned, she took out of her lap a foot-long embossed leather object and slowly pulled out a long dagger with an elaborate carving on the handle.

"The Comyn Sgian-dubh," she said slowly.

"Oh, really, Mother," Caroline said.

"Tell us, please, what is the significance of the knife?" José asked.

"It's a dagger, passed down from father to son for generations."

"I've never seen it before," Allan said.

"One wears the sgian-dubh in one's stocking as a personal weapon and this may be the only remaining relic of The Red Comyn and The Black Comyn."

"If it's passed down from father to son, why is it we've never seen it before?"

"Because it's not from the Browne side. It's from the Comyns, from mine."

"And where did you get it, pray tell?" Caroline asked.

"You'll hear soon enough. But first, I'll tell you the significance of this sgian-dubh. When one is asked a question, the answer must be the truth or there are dire consequences."

"Such as?" Fred asked. He seemed as perplexed by this object as we were, and he picked it up to examine it more carefully.

I got the impression that she was making things up as she went along, and I glanced at John, whose quirked eyebrow suggested he felt the same way.

"How do you know if someone is telling the truth?" Joan asked.

"I don't have to. The dagger knows."

"Okay, I'm game," Allan said, looking at his watch conspicuously. It seemed he wanted to humor his mother but not spend too much time doing it.

"First, I'll spin it, and to whomever it points will be the first to respond."

The carved knife was spun, and the blade stopped at José. He smiled and looked expectantly.

"Do you intend to stay in this country?" Hextilda asked.

He laughed. "There would be dire consequences, as you put it, if I said no. But in all honesty, I say yes."

"Good answer, sir," Fred commented to scattered light laughter.

"Again," Hextilda said, giving the dagger a turn with her hand and the blade pointed at me.

"Who are you most jealous of?"

I wasn't by nature but knew I had to give an answer. "There was another student in nursing school who always did better than I on every test." I looked around for a reaction at my very dull answer but there were polite smiles.

Fred got the point next.

"What was your biggest fear as a child?"

"I can say without hesitation, it was that bear in the dining room."

"Me, too," Caroline said.

The dagger spun again and pointed toward John. He gulped.

"Have you ever hit something or someone with your car?"

He hesitated. "Aside from a curb or two, no. Well, there was a deer in Colorado, once. It ran off so I don't know how injured it was."

Joan was the next target.

"Do you have a favorite child?"

"Isn't that a question that we should ask of you?" Joan replied.

"Is that your answer?"

Joan said nothing else but smiled.

Allan was the next to have the dagger stop before him. "What is one thing you would do if there were no consequences?"

He stood up and pointed at his mother. "I would stop this stupid game right now and go up to bed." He pushed at the table so hard the dagger slid off and landed at the floor at his mother's feet.

Then the arguing began and John, José and I slipped out of the room closing the door as the sharp voices escalated and accusations were hurled. For the sake of decency, José led John and me to the other end of the hall where there was a library, soft chairs and a chessboard set out. The two men looked at each other, nodded, sat down and began. Their calm suited me and to take my mind off the hum of drama two rooms away, I decided to peruse the shelves to get a sense of the family's taste in reading.

Not surprisingly, someone was or had been a military enthusiast as there were sets of books about the Revolutionary War, battles and leaders of the Revolutionary War, the Seven Years War, the English Civil War, the American Civil War, along with continental wars of which I had never heard, such as the Polish Ottoman War. I tried to imagine how these two entities became engaged in conflict since in modern times they were geographically far apart, but just to make sure, I walked to the globe on its stand in the corner and confirmed that I was not as ignorant as I thought. Poland is up near the Baltic, with many countries in between before reaching the Ottoman empire, so I could only imagine both entities were likely larger in the past.

I returned to the bookcase to see more familiar items, such as the works of Edgar Allen Poe, Montaigne, Voltaire and a long string of books entitled *Courtiers and Favourites of Royalty*. I didn't doubt that there were enough to fill that many tomes but was surprised that any one person could have researched the topic that spanned many centuries. I flipped through some volumes and found a hefty chapter about Diane de Poitiers, reclined on the sofa and began to read.

We heard doors opening and closing, others slamming, before all was quiet in the downstairs rooms and before I knew it, the whiskey and wine had me dozing off. I felt my shoulder being gently shaken and woke with a start looking into John's amused face.

"Aren't you the life of the party," he said, taking the book from where it lay and pulling me upright.

"Whew, too much alcohol," I said. We were alone in the library and the chess set was back in its original position, which meant I had been asleep for some time.

The Great Room was quiet, the lights dimmed and the fire burned low in the grate. It seemed the entire household had gone to bed, and we went to our separate rooms after a kiss goodnight. There was a small table lamp on the vanity leaving much of the room in shadow as I removed my jewelry and clothes and got into pajamas and bathrobe before going to the bathroom down the hall. I tiptoed in my slippers, which was silly since the carpeted gallery masked any noise, washed up quickly and looked forward to falling into the soft mattress and sleeping late.

When I opened the door to my room, I saw there was no light at all, and I was sure I hadn't turned the lamp off. Just to be sure, I turned the switch, and it came on. Somebody had been in here. I saw the pearls lying curled on the vanity top and wondered if one of the girls working here had come in and turned it off. An odd thought hit me, and I looked in the closet to see if anything had been touched or missing, as if I had anything worth taking. Everything was as I had left it less than ten minutes earlier.

I went to the bed to turn down the coverlet and saw it. The dagger. The sgian-dubh was lying on my pillow glittering at me.

I gasped. My heart was racing, not because I was scared, but because I was angry that someone thought this was an amusing idea. I picked it up and went down the hall to John's room and tapped on the door. No answer. I tapped again and he opened the door squinting in the half-light.

"What is it?"

I held the dagger up before him.

66

He shook his head, not understanding. I put my hand on his chest and gently pushed him back into his room.

"This was on my pillow just now," I said.

"What? Why?"

"I have no idea why, but this is the last straw." I plopped myself down on the end of his bed and looked up sternly. "I don't know who did it or why, but this family is poisonous."

He tried to shush me, and I lowered my voice.

"I put up with their nasty squabbling and Hextilda's absurd game that I'm sure she made up, just as she made up this whole Christmas thing, and I didn't enjoy being made fun of or humiliated. I would like to go home in the morning."

John shook his head as if to clear it.

"All right, we can do that. It will be awkward to think of a reason...."

"*This* is the reason," I said, holding up the dagger. "The preposterous thing that she was trying to pass off as an antique that has magical powers. And we all just sat there like stupid pigeons, too intimidated to call her on it."

John sighed. "You're right. Let's talk in the morning, okay?"

I got up, still angry and not mollified by John's appeasement. By the time I got back to my room, I felt a little guilty waking him up but still not confident of my safety, I checked that the closet held only my clothes, and nobody was lurking under the bed. I put the dagger next to my pearls on the vanity, turned to lock the door and put the vanity chair up against it in the event someone had a key, then rolled myself into bed, hoping to calm down enough to sleep.

Chapter Nine

I awoke with a piercing headache, got dressed and looked over the gallery railing to see John alone in the Great Room below waiting for me. He stood as I came into view, and I sat in the chair next to him.

"What do you want to do?" he asked.

"I'd very much like to leave. But first, breakfast, and I'd like to return this to Hextilda." I held out the dagger wrapped in a silk scarf I had brought.

He made a face of disappointment and nodded his head before we made our way to the dining room, now brightly lit without the looming shadows of antlers and stuffed animal heads.

There was a sideboard with a chafing dish of scrambled eggs, plates of sausages and bacon, and a bread basket of scones and muffins. The stern mood I was attempting to maintain lessened at the sight of such a hearty meal and I heaped my plate.

We had just sat down and poured coffee for ourselves when Hextilda came into the room, all smiles.

"I trust you slept well?" she asked.

I unwrapped the silk scarf. "This was left on my pillow."

"There it is! Oh, I have been looking all over for it." She held out her hand with a thankful smile.

"It was left on my pillow," I repeated.

Now she looked concerned. "But what can that mean? Do you think someone was trying to frighten you? And why?"

"We thought it best if we leave today, if you don't mind," John said mildly.

"You can't! That would be terrible. What sort of a hostess would I be to let that happen?"

She stood in front of us, and tears welled in her eyes.

"I'm sorry," I said, but I was not going to back down.

She left the room quickly and I looked at John. "I feel terrible, but...."

"Don't worry, let me bring the car around to the front and after breakfast, we'll pack and load it up."

I didn't tell him that I had already packed everything but my washbag. We ate in silence and once done, he went to attend to the car, and I waited in the Great Room where a fire was warming the room. He was gone longer than I imagined it would take to drive from the covered parking area to the front of the house and when he came back in, he looked annoyed.

"The battery is dead. The car won't start."

"How is that possible?" I knew he took impeccable care of his car since it was often needed for late-night house visits and had to be reliable transportation.

"I looked for Bruce for some assistance to jump start it, but he has gone to town with Allan and no one else seems to know where jumper cables are. I'll wait for Fred to be up and ask him for help."

The young girl, Mariah, came in at that moment. "Doctor Taylor, Doctor Fred is in the library, and he may be able to help." She looked sorry to have delivered any bad news and backed out of the room.

John left in search of his friend and returned a few minutes later.

"Fred's here and willing to help but he doesn't have any jumper cables and doesn't know where any are. So, your notion of getting out of here soon is not going to happen. I don't know why my car won't start, but I don't for an instant think Hextilda had anything to do with that."

"I don't, either. Since we can't leave, we may as well change into sturdy clothes and...."

"Walk back to the highway?" John asked.

"No, take a long walk around the grounds. Get out in the air and clear my head. Maybe yours could do with some fresh air, too. Let's ask Fred to show us around."

* * *

I hadn't realized how vast the property was until we were out trekking through it. When John and I had driven down the long path to the house just yesterday, we could glimpse part of a small lake some distance from the house to the south beyond a large, wooded area. Judging by the direction Fred was taking us, we might come upon it after going through those woods crossed with several paths that were probably man-made.

"Do you own this entire valley?" John asked.

Fred looked a bit embarrassed. "My father made bucketfuls of money in finance and the stock market."

"I thought you had a house in Boston, too," I said.

"Yes, on Beacon Hill. John has been there a few times, but none of the family were present."

I breathed in the cold air that smelled of balsam pines, the scent of Christmas trees for me. I walked until I found a smallish one, broke off a branch and rubbed the needles between my bare hands.

"Just smell that!"

John leaned over and inhaled. "I think I'm going to enjoy Christmas this year," he said.

I looked at him in a puzzled way. "This Christmas, here?"

"No, I mean the holiday with your family. My celebration last year was a pity invitation from Miss Manley, which I appreciated but which made me feel even more disconnected. I gave her some stationery and a bottle of Sherry, and she gave me a hand-knitted scarf. I probably should have stayed home and listened to the radio."

Fred laughed. "Oh, you poor, lonely soul. I had invited you to Boston, remember?"

"Yes, but I couldn't refuse my neighbor."

"If you were her only guest, you were doing her a favor, too," I said.

"I wasn't the only guest. Stuart was there, going on about all the society people he knew who were giving New Year's Eve parties—those he was invited to and those he hoped to 'swing an invite to,' as he put it. The only respite was Glenda popping by with her mother."

"Oh, dear, her last Christmas," I sighed. Then I thought of having to spend a long meal with Stuart. I never did understand what Glenda saw in him.

"Who is he?" Fred asked.

"My landlady's nephew. He is an author and in the publishing business. Hudson-Manley."

Fred shrugged. "Never heard of him. Publishing is a rough business. I am surprised my mother has kept at it all these years. Although it has been lucrative, I think she is getting tired of it."

"Is that why she was fishing around for something different to write?"

"Perhaps. Maybe she's getting tired of pulling Alistair out of all his predicaments or thinking of those obstacles in the first place."

We arrived at a fork in the path. "Which way shall we go?" Fred asked and John pointed to the right. We walked in silence as the path sloped downwards and the wind became colder and damper and I wished we could see the sky for impending rain or snow but the trees blocked our view. A woodpecker drummed on a branch somewhere, its noise the only sound we heard other than our own footsteps.

Ahead, down the long winding trail, we could see a patch of blue through the trees and several minutes later the path widened, and we were standing at the edge of a sizeable lake. Off to the left, partly obscured by trees was a boathouse with a small pier projecting over the water.

We stumbled over rocks to get to it and saw a path leading back up into the woods.

"If you had chosen the left fork back there, we could have saved ourselves some trouble," Fred said, holding his hand out to me as I negotiated a slippery boulder.

"I took the one less traveled by, and that has made all the difference," I quoted.

It didn't look like anyone had been out here in some time as the paint was peeling off the trim of the one window we could see from our side. Standing on tiptoe, Fred cleaned the cobwebs off the window with his hand as John peered inside.

"A canoe and a rowboat. And a lot more cobwebs."

I walked around toward the back of the wooden structure to a door and pulled it open to what must be the tackle room, closed off to the elements and the boats on the other end. I expected to see ropes, buoys, and oars and paddles, which I did, but there was also a makeshift bed on the floor consisting of bundles of blankets. It could just be rags that someone had left here but there was definitely a pillow of ticking material and looking further on the horizontal supports someone had used like shelves a box of matches and an empty, crumpled package of Lucky Strike cigarettes.

"What's this?" John asked.

Fred came up behind him. "I don't know. Some children's hide-out? Some young people sneaking a smoke?"

"Somebody's emergency dwelling? Like the person we saw in the woods when we first drove up?"

"You didn't tell me about that," Fred said.

"I didn't know if it was a hobo or just someone walking through the woods...."

"Or a bear," John added, smiling at me.

There was another door just opposite to where we stood, and

John opened it, revealing the part of the boathouse where the canoe and rowboat were stored.

"Whoever it was could have started a fire," Fred said. "This old wooden building would go up in minutes."

We turned back to the door at the rear.

"Does anyone in the family come down here?" I asked.

"Judging from the dust, I would guess no one has gone out on either craft in a long time."

We decided to walk along the rocky shore to the far end of the lake, where a few ducks were floating and a medium-size structure of branches and sticks projected from the bank.

"Look, a beaver dam!" John said.

I had never seen one in nature, and I wanted to see the beavers, but it seemed the increasing cold and murky sky was keeping them warm in their den.

"Yes, my father was an engineer at heart. He made sure to get some beavers in here who dammed up the stream and we got a lake to boat on and swim in."

I tried to keep up with the longer strides of the men and stumbled over the root of a tree and fell onto my knees. It didn't hurt much since I was wearing woolen pants with long underwear underneath, but my dignity was injured. Had I not fallen, I wouldn't have seen the piece of leather sticking out of the water, caught by a stray branch.

As John backtracked to help pull me up, I pointed to it.

"Either someone lost a glove or that's the leather cover to the sgian-dubh," I said.

Fred came back and fished it out of the shallow water with a stick and we all saw the embossed leather, no longer a warm brown but dark from its partial immersion in the lake.

"It is."

We looked at one other. "John, I'm thinking the person who put the dagger on my pillow was the person who threw this case into the lake."

"The only people who know their way around this property are my family."

"Yes, the family and the people who work here. And they would have to find their way out here in the dark. The only people who wouldn't know how to do that, are José...."

"Possibly."

"And you and I. So that doesn't help very much," John said.

We retraced our steps as the wind stopped blowing, but before we had even got halfway back to the path up out of the woods, the snow began. Like a child, I laughed at the huge flakes that soon covered the knit caps on our heads and we regained the shelter of the woods and walked quickly back toward the house. When we came out of the forest a half hour later, I was shocked to see that this was a full-blown snowstorm, and we could hardly see the castle through the blizzard in progress except that the house was dark brown and could be glimpsed intermittently when a gust died down. No matter, Fred was with us and certainly could lead us back safely.

We reached the back entrance to the castle where there was paving and stomped our feet to get most of the snow off, shook our heads and wiped down our coats, only to be covered a few moments later by more snow. Luckily the door was unlocked, and we came into a mudroom where boots, coats and hats were stored and quickly made puddles on the floor as we began to take ours off.

Eleanor came to the doorway to the kitchen and looked us up and down.

"Storm's a big one. Bruce and Mr. Allan are still out in it some-where." That's all she said before returning to her work.

Chapter Ten

Our outer clothes were soaked through and taking them off I found that my sweater, blouse, pants, everything was completely wet including the sodden knit cap. Leaving the boots behind, we walked through the kitchen and found ourselves in the hallway next to the dining room and close to the staircase to the second floor.

"I think we're leaving footprints behind," I said, turning to confirm my suspicion. At least I knew that I would get my soak in that huge bathtub I had seen yesterday. Not ten minutes later I was doing just that, the vapor rising from the water, my toes wriggling in the warmth, thinking of how I would spend the rest of the day. Then I stopped myself—we were going to go back home but the lack of a functioning battery in the car, no assistance in recharging it and now a raging snowstorm—we were going to be here today, probably tomorrow and perhaps even longer if the weather continued. Well, aside from the strange family dynamics, and someone's idea of a joke on me, one could be stranded in much worse circumstances. We had electricity, hot water, heat, food and plenty of books to read.

After I had dressed and dried my hair as best I could with

repeated rubbing with a towel while I leaned over the radiator, I looked out the bedroom window and found I could not see much of anything except white. I rubbed the pane with my hand thinking my vision was impaired by condensation, but no, it was an all-encompassing blizzard the likes of which I had never experienced. Glenda had told me they had often been snowed in when she grew up in West Adams, but I assumed she was exaggerating at first and then teasing me since she knew that's where I would be this year. Now I knew she probably hadn't made it up.

I took Hextilda's book and left my room, concerned that I didn't have a key to lock it from the outside and then had the brilliant idea of reading in the Great Room below seated near the fireplace in a chair with a view of the gallery. If anyone came or went from those rooms, I could see and probably hear them.

The first person I spotted was John, newly bathed with his clothes changed, carrying a book and heading toward the inner staircase. He sat down in a massive armchair on the other side of the fire and looked content.

"What are you reading?" I asked.

"Don't tell Fred, but I found this book on chess in their library. I guess it's not cheating, but I have been out of practice."

"I'm sure there is someone in West Adams who would enjoy a game with you. Reverend Lewis?"

"That's a good idea. I was going to ask if you...."

"No, John. I think engaging in a competitive endeavor would be a bad idea."

He looked somewhat wounded, made a scoffing noise and opened his book.

It was deliciously quiet and warm there, but I was not going to succumb to another impromptu nap. As it turned out, there was no possibility as Hextilda burst into the room from one of the archways with a broad smile at seeing us.

"I was so worried! I thought perhaps you got lost on your walk this morning."

"We were on our way back to the house and suddenly the storm was upon us," John said.

"Do you usually get blizzards this early?" I asked.

"We certainly get snow, but this one is unusually heavy. It's still coming down and it isn't even noon yet. My concern is that Bruce and Allan went off this morning—heaven knows why or to where, and they aren't back yet."

"Perhaps they stopped where they were and are waiting it out," I suggested.

"I hope not. With a storm like this, we could be socked in for days."

My heart sank. I was reconciled to another day here but not multiple days.

"Is the storm just local or is it regional?" John asked. "I bet if we listen to the radio, we could get some information."

"There's one in the sitting room," Hextilda said, pointing him in that direction; however, she didn't accompany him.

Turning to me she said, "I want to apologize for my behavior last evening."

"That's quite all right," I fibbed.

She sat down in the chair that John had just vacated. "You know I had confided in Fred that I thought someone was trying to kill me and I'm afraid all those ridiculous machinations with the dagger and truth-telling last night were my attempt to ferret out who it could be."

"If I may ask, why do you think someone is out to kill you? And why do you think it is someone in your family?"

"Who else cares enough to send them? Some farmer?"

"Have you shown Fred the notes? By the way you are talking now, there must have been more than the one you showed us when we were first here. Did you keep any of the others?"

"Yes, would you like to see them?" Hextilda asked.

Naturally, I would since I was incurably curious and now felt sorry for the poor woman.

She led me out to the archway near the dining room and along the hall to her study at the end.

"My inner sanctum," she said, dramatically.

At one of the facing desks was a woman who stopped typing as we entered.

"Hello. Would you like me to leave?" she asked.

"Oh, I don't think you've met each other yet," Hextilda said and introduced us. "Why don't you take a break?" she suggested to her secretary.

"I can't stand the clatter of typing," Hextilda whispered after she left. "That's why we work with dictation from me and shorthand on her part. She types up the day's work and I review it with changes before the end of the day."

"That sounds like quite an efficient production."

"Yes, well, if I weren't so disorganized," she said shuffling through papers on one of the desks. She stopped a few times, muttering and setting what looked like a bill to the side and another piece of paper got balled up and thrown into the trash bin.

"Oh, dear. I don't know where I put it. Perhaps I can get it for you later."

"Certainly," I responded, not sure why she wanted me to see it in the first place except to excuse her strange behavior of the evening before.

I made my way back to the Great Room but not seeing John there, I found him in the sitting room perched on a footstool, his head cocked toward the large radio. He held his hand up as I came in as the crackling voice and intermittent silences made little intelligible sense. He turned it off and got up.

"I was able to catch part of a report from Burlington that said the entire state and Northeast was getting blasted by some arctic air and they expected a significant snowfall."

"Expected?" I guess they haven't heard from anyone around here. Just look at it! You can't make out anything except white. Where did Bruce and Allan go this morning? Any idea?"

"I didn't see them this morning and I can't imagine where they went."

"Perhaps like us they just thought it was an overcast winter's day. It didn't look very much like a snow sky when we started out."

"Did you happen to tell Hextilda about the dagger case we found by the lake?"

"No, I didn't have a chance. She wanted me to see more of threatening notes she had received that started all this anxiety in the first place except she couldn't put her hands on them."

John looked past my shoulder and I turned to see someone standing in the doorway.

"Oh, Mariah, you're still here," I said, then apologized for sounding tactless as I realized it was not she.

"I'm her cousin, Nancy. We're here for the weekend and with the storm as it is perhaps longer. Mrs. Mowbray is calling everyone to luncheon," she said, leaving abruptly.

We trooped into the dining room and Caroline, José and Joan, who were already seated, nodded to us. It was only then that I wondered where they had been all morning, certainly not traipsing around in the snow.

José turned the tables on me with, "What were you all doing this morning? Eleanor said you had gone for a walk."

"And brought a blizzard back with you," Joan commented.

Fred laughed. "It was a gorgeous day when we started, only turning treacherous on our way back. Where's Allan?"

"He went with Bruce into town for something. I'm getting worried that they skidded off the road or landed in a snowdrift."

"Ah, Joan, ever the optimist," Caroline said.

Hextilda came in, followed by Adele, who sat at her side as they continued to discuss some issue of punctuation. Caroline raised her eyebrows in irritation.

"I do hope there is enough food to last for the next few days." She looked at the two young women who brought in a large tureen of soup and put it on the sideboard. Nancy's face flushed, possibly thinking that the remark about shortages was due to additional help at the house but that did not stop the flow of her methodical ladling of soup into a bowl, passing it to Mariah, who placed it on a plate and delivered it to each of us in turn. It was a thick brown with small white objects barely visible in the liquid.

"Mutton barley soup," Hextilda said. "One of Mrs. Mowbray's specialties."

"I haven't had that in a long time," Caroline said, pushing her plate away and lighting a cigarette.

I thought of my brother, Eddie, who at that moment would have asked, "Are you finished?" It was his way of eating whatever was left on everyone else's plate, a habit my mother found barbaric.

"Not at the table, dear," her Hextilda said.

Caroline got up and left the table to smoke elsewhere.

Oh, good, I thought, *another pleasant family meal.*

The freshly baked rolls were passed around and it was a very brief meal as we ate in silence and at a rapid pace. From between spoonfuls, we looked at each other around the table to sense what remark or argument might occur and, in my case, what innocuous comment I could make to break the tension.

Joan excused herself and got up, followed by José, who nodded to Hextilda. I wasn't in need of company at that point, so I made a pretense of stifling a yawn and asking to be excused as well and went back to my room to read in peace. The heavy soup, the soft coverlet and the dim light were all I needed to doze off.

I awoke with a start, not that there was any noise or disturbance, and I turned to the window to see that it was still snowing and the sun was going down. I decided to be more visible and took my book downstairs to the sitting room and found everyone except Hextilda was there. I made a movement with my hand, indicating I would go elsewhere, but John encouraged me to stay, whether to join the gang or keep him company or act as a buffer if there were harsh words, but there must have been a détente at some point because all was calm. The conclusion that I came to was that it was their mother who somehow unleased squabbling or ill feelings, and since she wasn't present, the tone of the room was more relaxed. Caroline had been reading a magazine, José a book and Joan was busy poking a needle back and forth into an embroidery hoop.

"Have Bruce and Allan returned yet?" I asked.

Joan's pinched look told me that they had not.

"It's getting dark, and the snow is still coming down," she said.

"Don't worry," Fred reassured her. "Bruce is the most capable of men and Allan can hold his own, too."

She laughed darkly. "That's what I am afraid of." She continued her work and John gave me a side glance to indicate that things had not been as calm as I had thought.

"What's that you are reading?" Caroline asked.

"Your mother's first book, *Romance in the Heather*."

Caroline rolled her eyes. "Introducing the dreadfully randy Alistair."

"I guess I haven't got to that part yet," I said laughing. "Just now he is being chased by someone who is likely to be the nemesis in the story."

"My mother forbade me to read her books, which was a joke. After all, they were readily available around the house and several girls at my school had them. In fact, it boosted my popularity that my mother could know all about such things. By the time I got to read any of them, I was disappointed that they were so tame."

"Tame? What other stuff were you reading?" Fred asked.

"I'd rather not say," she answered, closing her eyes in disdain.

"That entire Scottish thing was Daddy's strange obsession to begin with. Then Mother decided that she was related to the Comyn clan, which I highly doubt, and she rechristened herself Hextilda, based on some historical Scottish woman. Her real name is Hilda, you know."

Joan dropped her work into her lap and laughed too loudly. "Yes, no common name for her!"

I thought it was a rather interesting name.

"Don't be daft, Caroline," Fred said. "It's a pen name. It has much more flair that Hilda Browne, you must admit."

She shrugged her shoulders in begrudging acknowledgment.

"I've lived in this country since I was very small and I have never understood the fascination with the Scots," José said. "For all that Americans emulate the English, it seems odd to me that they are enamored by the ruffians to the north."

I laughed. "Oh, I thought you were referring to Canadians."

"No, to the north of England," he corrected me, smiling. He was an extraordinarily handsome man with his dark hair, fair skin and brilliantly white teeth.

"They have lived for centuries feeling oppressed and Americans love rooting for the underdog. And we are a cheerful race and Scots are dour. They even pronounce it 'do-wer' to emphasize how bad it is. Opposites attract," Joan said.

I thought it strange that Joan classified herself amongst the cheerful as she sat there, a scornful look on her face, jabbing the embroidery needle into the linen cloth.

Eleanor appeared at the door to the sitting room. "Someone's coming up to the house. I hope it's Bruce." She turned and Joan put down her needlework and followed. We all got up to make sure that it was Bruce and Allan and crowded toward the entry in the Great Room.

There was scraping of booted feet outside the front door and Bruce came in, accompanied by a man. Joan gasped, whether in relief or dismay, then realized it was not her husband. It was a young man with cheeks red from the harsh weather, dressed in heavy wool from head to toe, bearing an embarrassed look as he entered and stood to the side while Allan assisted someone else from the car who hopped on one foot, holding the other one up to protect it. They came into the foyer dripping their wet clothes onto the slate floor while we gaped at them. The latest arrival looked up, took off her knitted hat and said in a conversational tone, "Hello."

Chapter Eleven

She held out her hand. "Julia Morris. This is my brother Kent."

"I'm so sorry for the intrusion, but we were hiking and suddenly the weather started to get bad, so we made our way back to the main road," he said, his face getting red.

"I stupidly twisted my ankle, and it took us forever to get back to the road. And then nobody was driving on it anyway because of the storm."

"We had a devil of a time even finding what looked like a road with all the snow piling up so quickly. Thank God for Mr. Mowbray and Mr. Browne chugging along slowly in their truck, or we would have been run over." Kent tried for a laugh.

"Oh, Allan! What were you thinking?" Joan said, pushing herself between her husband and the young woman he was partly holding upright. Kent moved and put an arm around his sister, looking uncomfortable.

"Well, then. Let's get organized. We haven't introduced ourselves, have we? I am Hextilda Cumming Browne, this is my eldest son, Frederick, you've met Allan, this is his wife Joan, my daughter Caroline, her friend José, John Taylor, a family friend, and Aggie Burnside.

Now, John, could you look at Julia's ankle? Bruce, please ask Eleanor to make up another room for these two young people."

Bruce scowled.

"All right then, perhaps Julia could share with Aggie? The room is made up and wouldn't it be nice to have your nurse in attendance?"

"Excellent suggestion," John said.

"Kent can bunk with José," Hextilda went on, not asking José if that was acceptable. She looked the men up and down as if measuring them up. "Fred, surely you have some extra warm clothing that Kent could wear. If not, there must be something of Daddy's lying about. Caroline, what can you rustle up something for Julia to wear?"

It was a noisy event, with Joan admonishing Allan for being away and in danger, Kent and Julia both protesting about the intrusion and imposition while simultaneously thanking Hextilda for her generosity, and Caroline grumbling about having to dig in the back of her closet for the unexpected guest.

"Chop, chop!" came Hextilda's familiar command for everyone to get moving and do as they had been instructed.

John and I helped Julia over to the couch in the Great Room and she gingerly removed her boot onto the Persian carpet. It was a good thing Eleanor was not in the room or she would have had a fit over that sight. Then very slowly and carefully, John removed the thick sock that revealed an ankle that didn't look very swollen yet, although there was a bruise on one side.

She sucked air between her teeth in an effort not to cry out as he gently pressed around the perimeter searching for signs of bone damage.

"Sorry, this is going to hurt a bit." He prodded a bit more and she grimaced.

"I don't think anything is broken, probably just twisted. But once we get it bandaged up and elevated, it should feel a lot better."

I felt a presence, which was Eleanor scowling down at the puddle around the boot on the rug, then she looked up to meet Hextilda's inquiring look.

"Do we have one of those elastic socks?"

"An ACE bandage would be better if you have one," John said.

"I've got one upstairs somewhere," Fred volunteered.

"Do you have anything for pain?" John asked to Fred's retreating back.

"Yes," he answered over his shoulder. "Tincture of opium. That will work."

"Do you think you will need anything?" John asked the young woman.

"Yes, I'm afraid I have a low pain tolerance."

Allan appeared at her elbow. "This could be all you need," he said, offering her a glass of whiskey that she gratefully accepted.

"Let's all have a drink," he said. "To warm up from the weather and celebrate finding two wandering souls in the storm."

Eleanor produced a tray with glasses, set it down with a bit of a bang and retreated to the kitchen. No ice for this toast as the young people looked cold enough despite still having their coats on.

"Where were you hiking to exactly?" I asked.

"We pulled off the main road onto the shoulder and parked. We were trying to get back to the same place on the road but couldn't see where we were going with the blinding storm."

He hadn't answered my question and it wasn't important. I just thought it odd to pick a random spot to park your vehicle and then wander into the woods, for surely that was all there was around here on either side of the road, no hills with notable views.

"I bet your poor car will be practically invisible and covered with a foot of snow."

"If the snowplows come through it might be even harder to dig it out. What a stupid thing to have done, I know."

They shrugged off their coats and scarves and I was surprised to see that although they both had on high turtlenecks, sweaters and wool pants, it seemed like more casual wear than what was usual for a long hike on a cold day. I became more curious about where they had come from and where they were going but decided to leave that for later.

"Come on, we'll help you upstairs," I said to Julia.

"Allan, I bet we still have that pair of crutches up in the attic. Would you have a look?" Hextilda asked.

He gulped down the remainder of his drink and went out to the stairs, across the gallery and disappeared down the far end. We managed to get Julia up on one foot, made sure she was steady and then made our way slowly across the floor to the archway leading to the stairs.

"We probably should have left her downstairs and brought the warm clothes to her," John said, and I agreed but we were already several steps upward and decided to continue.

"At least she'll have some privacy up here."

We got her onto the second bed in my room and John left me to help her get undressed and under the covers while waiting for a change of clothes.

"Are you a real nurse?" she asked.

"Yes, I am a real nurse. So, in my official capacity, I can ask, how are you feeling?"

She laughed a bit. "I feel stupid for getting into this situation in the first place. It was my idea to go hiking and I dragged my brother along."

"Why here?"

"I heard this part of Vermont was beautiful and we were just in Burlington and heading back to New York City."

That made no sense whatsoever since Burlington was on the other side of the state, but I let her ramble on.

"How am I feeling? Actually, a little tipsy. I think I drank that whiskey too quickly."

"Would you like some water? There is a small pitcher here."

She nodded, I poured a glass for her and decided to leave the questions to someone else.

A knock on the door and Caroline opened it a crack to ask if she could come in. She had a large bundle in her arms and let it tumble onto the bed.

"Mother likes us to dress for dinner, but I thought we could grant you a reprieve under the circumstances. Here's a cashmere sweater—not my color at all—and a jumper that was my mother's, probably too large for you, but it will keep you warm and here are some tights. Well, that won't work if you can't put them on over your foot and the bandage. Wait, here are some thick socks. Quite an outfit!"

"Thank you, it will be perfect."

"There's a flannel nightgown, too, and someone will bring up a pair of shoes, well, let's say a shoe, that should work."

"Thank you," Julia said, biting her lip as if to not to cry.

"Just another day at Browne's Castle," Caroline said, leaving.

"Browne's Castle? Is that where we are?"

I asked if Julia needed help getting dressed and she said no, although she struggled with the sock over her bandaged foot. The clothes seemed large and strange on her, especially when I reached in the closet to get out my new blue dress.

"Oh, I can't join you all for dinner like this," she said seeing what was in my arms.

"If we can get you downstairs, you should, otherwise Eleanor will have to send up a tray and I don't think she'll be pleased."

"Is she rather a dragon?"

"Let's just say she keeps everyone in line."

I changed my clothes, my stockings and shoes and listened to Julia admiring the new dress. Hair combed, pearls in place and I helped her to sit up.

"Let me see about those shoes and the crutches, although please don't try to go down- or upstairs with them. It's very dangerous unless you are practiced at it."

Ten minutes later the footgear and crutches were in our hands and Allan assisted me in getting the new patient down the hall and the stairway and into the Great Room. Mariah stepped into the room and banged on a gong to let us know that dinner would be served shortly.

"Time for just another short tot," Allan said, looking in my direction. I declined, Julia accepted, and he poured himself more than a bit. The rest of the company assembled shortly and were very jolly knowing that four people, two presumed missing and two newly found, were here in a warm house, having a drink and about to have what I assumed would be another luxurious meal.

"Oh, here's Adele, my assistant," Hextilda said as the woman hastily entered the room patting down her hair.

"My apologies. The ribbon got all twisted," she said looking at the remaining ink stain on her hands from the typewriter.

"Let's hope it holds up—we don't know how long until we can get to town to get another."

They instinctively looked up at the large window in the Great Room, but large flakes still came down from the sky as if it would never stop snowing.

"So, tell me, where have you all come from today?" Hextilda asked.

Kent looked at his sister and answered for them both, "We were outside of Burlington and thought to come west and south, maybe spending the night somewhere around here."

"There is no 'around here' here," Fred said. "Except Stamford and there is nowhere to stay there either, unless you pound on some farmer's door."

Kent blushed. "Well, city folks like us always think there will be a hotel or a restaurant nearby." He laughed at his own joke.

"What city are you from?" José asked.

"Manhattan, actually," Kent answered.

"Lovely, that's where I live as well. Eastside? Westside?"

"Midtown," he answered.

That was an odd answer. New Yorkers invariably mentioned

what street or avenue they lived on; it was a way of identifying who you were and who you knew.

"Lots going on there. I have an art gallery downtown. You must come to see it," Caroline offered. She ignored her mother's disdainful look at the mention of her business. "We have shows at least once a month."

"I don't know much about art," Kent responded.

"No matter, we love having a packed house. Artists can be so unrealistic about their work and if we don't have enough people show up, they can be depressed for days. We always have hors d'oeuvres, too." She winked.

"In that case...," he laughed at her comment.

"For heaven's sake, Kent. You'd think we needed to stand in a soup line or something," Julia said. She sat in an armchair with her foot balanced on an ottoman.

"I've never known such a storm, but then I'm not usually here so late in the season," Hextilda said. "But, once you're on a roll with writing, it's a good idea to keep going. I expect we'll be done with a good first draft in a week. Deadlines," she added in a mutter.

Eleanor appeared in the archway announcing dinner and all went in except Hextilda, who held me back for a moment.

"Do you think they are really brother and sister?" Hextilda asked me.

I stammered out an answer. "They do resemble each other. Dark hair and that flush to their cheeks when flustered."

"I'm not sure. That's why I created those sleeping arrangements, splitting them up." She took my arm and we proceeded through the archway.

I couldn't help but add, "Aha, very clever. But I will say that something is fishy about those two."

Chapter Twelve

Walking into the dining room, Hextilda once again became the cheerful hostess, making sure there were the usual alternating male-female seating arrangements but not placing couples together and allowing Julia to sit at the end where her foot could be propped up by another chair.

Kent looked at the ornamentation in the room and the multi-tiered candelabra on the table and said, "It's quite grand."

"No, it's not. It is entirely over the top. As am I. And as was their father, the late Mr. Browne who dreamed up this décor."

"Did he hunt these animals himself?" Kent asked.

"Some, yes, others were Allan's contribution and then we had to even out the display, so some were purchased. But what is more important to let you both know is that even though it is not December twenty-fifth, we are having a sort of Christmas this weekend."

The two newcomers looked surprised.

"I'm calling it my Ersatz Christmas," Hextilda said, holding up her glass of wine to initiate a toast. We all held up our glasses, even Joan who would not partake, and Allan being last to hold his up, looked uncomfortable and avoided eye contact with the rest of us.

"Merry Christmas!" Hextilda warbled.

"Merry Christmas!" we responded and took a sip of the burgundy.

Like some medieval feast, Bruce led the procession of food into the dining room, carrying what had to be a haunch of venison, followed by his wife with a smaller platter of game hens, then Mariah and Nancy bringing in bowls of vegetables. This weekend had been full of firsts for me but surely the food was of the likes I probably would never taste again.

Following the convention, we chatted to the seatmate to the right while the meat was being carved, which led me to ask Fred if he was a hunter like his father and brother.

"Fishing is about as far as I go," he said. He had such a mild, calm manner that I could easily imagine him sitting on a riverbank, gazing into the water waiting for that first bite. In contrast, I could see Allan, with his gruff manner, stalking game in a competition to bring home the biggest and best animal.

John was seated directly across from me and was smiling from ear to ear. I cocked my head to the side as if to ask *why* but he just continued smiling before being drawn into a conversation with Caroline.

"I hope Mother doesn't expect us to sing carols," Fred said.

"I love Christmas carols," I said with honest enthusiasm. "In Pelham, we have a town square, and midway through December the mayor lights the tree and we all sing carols."

"If this snow doesn't let up, you'll be doing that here. And spending New Year's Eve as well, judging by the pile-up outside."

The venison was like nothing I had eaten before in texture or flavor and it was not gamey, the criticism one often heard about wild meat. Julia was poking at her serving with her fork as if uncertain whether she was going to eat it and Allan, who was trying not to look at her but kept peering up through his eyebrows, finally spoke.

"That was shot right here on our grounds. I can assure you it is perfectly safe to eat."

She tried a bite and smiled at him and then Hextilda, who glanced over at me as if to suggest that she still thought something was off about the young woman.

"What is it you do, Kent?" she asked him.

He was mid-bite and paused to chew and swallow. "I'm a teacher."

"Really, where?"

"At a private academy in Manhattan. It's a small, progressive school. I teach English...."

"As did I," Hextilda said.

"And civics, too." He dove into his meal as if to halt the conversation.

"What do our young people think of the state of the world these days?" she asked.

"I only came on the faculty this year after my finance job fell through because of the Crash. A lot of the families of students had big losses as well. I'm lucky to have a job."

"What I meant was, do your students debate how to change the world? How they would have done something differently to prevent or help people out of poverty and hopelessness?"

Kent seemed baffled by the question and gave some half-baked response that, even though the students were privileged, they still had compassion for others. It didn't satisfy Hextilda's requirement for conversation, so she turned to her left where John sat, and they had a lively exchange about international politics. I was now obliged to have a conversation with my tablemate to the left, who was Kent, and I was stumped at how to begin.

"What do you do?" he asked me, allowing me to rattle on about the two medical practices that John had and my part in attending to the needs of the community. It was rough going and I was glad when the meal came to an end, the dishes were removed, and Hextilda asked us if we were ready for her next holiday game.

"Now, my family knows that I like to have our entertainment in the

Game Room, but in deference to our guest who has been jostled around enough already, we'll stay here. Last night, we had a Dundee cake with a little bairn hidden inside and our Joan was the one to have luck for the next year." She smiled broadly at her sour daughter-in-law. "That was something that I borrowed from the Louisiana custom for Twelfth Night. "Tonight, we have another borrowed custom of fortune cookies." She paused. "When Mariah brings them in," she added tartly, the timing of her performance thrown off because the dessert had not yet arrived.

Nancy entered with a pot of coffee and Mariah trailed behind with a stack of triangular-shaped cookies piled high in a bowl. She placed the bowl in the center of the table while she set plates out before each of us.

"I saw these in San Francisco last year on a book tour and I thought what a fun idea. Except I call them Bard cookies."

"Bar cookies?" Julia asked.

"No. Bard, as in Shakespeare. But instead of telling your fortune, these cookies will give you a phrase or quotation and you have to either identify it or expound upon it. My family knows I was an English teacher, and I just can't help myself."

Kent looked around the table for a further explanation of what this game entailed and he wasn't the only one. However, we all smiled, and she held her hand out to John, indicating that he should begin. He looked a bit dubious as he took the topmost cookie and Hextilda instructed him to break it open. Out popped a small piece of paper and he read aloud:

"*Now is the winter of our discontent.* Yes, times could certainly be better, but as Richard the Third continued, '*Made glorious summer by this sun of York*' putting in a pun about sun and son and I truly believe—even though it is indeed winter—that when summer comes, we will pull out of this difficult time."

"Happy Days Are Here Again?" Allan asked.

John turned a bit pink at the ribbing. "Yes, I think that is something that we all wish for. Don't you?"

93

"Hear, hear," Hextilda said. "I bet you can recite that entire soliloquy."

"Yes, but I won't bore you with it just now."

"Who's next? Let's try Joan."

She had to stand up to reach the bowl, chose a cookie and cracked it open with care. She read in silence and thought a moment before speaking. "'*Love looks not with the eyes but with the mind and therefore is winged Cupid painted blind.*' I wish I could remember which play it is from, but I can say with certainty that the sentiment is noble. One loves what is on the inside."

She sat down with a small smile on her face.

"My turn, I believe," José said. He split his confection and smiled. "How very apt! *The course of true love never did run smooth.*'" He laughed and Caroline blushed.

"I hope that didn't come from Romeo and Juliet," she said. "All did not end well there."

"I think you're making much ado about nothing," Fred said to a chorus of groans.

"That means you are next," Caroline said.

He opened his and laughed. "'*How sharper than a serpent's tooth it is to have a thankless child!*' King Lear—no explanation needed."

"I think that should have been mine," Hextilda said, but she was smiling.

"Do snakes have teeth?" Kent asked.

That paused the conversation for a moment.

"Not technically," John offered. "Fangs, of course, but that word would ruin the rhythm of the line."

"My turn," I said, hoping to choose something recognizable. "'*Cowards die many times before their deaths, the valiant never taste of death but once.*' I know that one: Julius Caesar, of course. '*Et Tu Brute.*'"

"Enough showing off, Aggie," John said, and I wrinkled my nose at him in mock distaste.

Allan leaned over to take a cookie from the middle of the stack sending the rest in disarray. "Sorry," he said, hastily putting them back in the bowl. "Mine is, '*Neither a borrower nor a lender be for loan oft loses both itself and friend.*' Hmm." He turned the paper over as if to find the answer. "I thought it was Ben Franklin who said that. And perhaps he did. A wise saying, nonetheless, and I will guess the Merchant of Venice."

"Tut, tut. It was Polonius lecturing his son before going off to university. I'm sure Daddy gave you much the same advice," Hextilda said.

Kent took his turn and laughed a bit. "'*Brevity is the soul of wit!*'" He held his hands out in triumph and said no more.

Fred clapped, "Very good, and lucky for you to get that."

"Hamlet," I whispered.

Caroline bit her lip nervously and settled on her choice. "'*The fault lies not within the stars, but in ourselves that we are underlings.*' Wait, something is missing. The fault... dear Brutus! That's it. Julius Caesar. Oh, if he only knew what was coming his way."

"Well done, darling," Hextilda said.

"Point to the one you'd like, and I'll get it for you," Allan said to Julia.

She gestured randomly and he handed a cookie to her.

"I'm not very good at games," she started before opening it with a crack. "'*False face must hide what the false heart doth know.*' That could be Julius Caesar, but we've had him already. Or Hamlet, but he was done, too."

"He was done, all right," Fred said.

"As was Caesar," John added.

"I'm going to guess Macbeth?" she asked.

Applause all around and Julia looked relieved.

"Adele, your turn."

"This isn't very fair since I made half of these, but here we go. '*Misery acquaints a man with strange bedfellows.*' I didn't create this one, but I recognize it from The Tempest."

"Isn't it, 'Misery Loves Company' or is that Ben Franklin again?" Allan asked.

"Marlowe, Doctor Faustus. Misery may love company, but you can ignore the invitation," Adele said.

"And now, for our hostess," John said. "Although I think you stacked the deck."

"I would never do such a thing," she smiled.

"The lady doth protest too much, methinks," he retorted.

"Don't worry. I'll let you know if I get one of my own, otherwise it won't be any fun."

The performance tension any of the guests had felt dissipated now that it was Hextilda's turn, and we were all smiling in anticipation of what convoluted quote she might get. She smiled in happy anticipation, cracked open the cookie, unfurled the paper and dropped the lot on the table with a horrible scowl.

"What is it?" John asked.

She didn't answer but scanned each of the faces around the table. John picked up the paper and read aloud, "'*All that live must die.*'"

Several gasps were heard, mine included.

"Is that a Shakespeare quote?" Kent asked.

"A rather mangled one," Hextilda said. "A tedious truism. Why did you include that one, Adele?"

"I didn't."

The room was very quiet.

"That's not funny at all," Hextilda said standing. The electric lights went out all at once leaving just the candles on the table burning, illuminating the harsh features of her angry face.

Chapter Thirteen

"Oh, we've lost power," Joan said. "What shall we do?"

"Nothing to be done," Allan responded. "We've got plenty of candles and I expect a raft of flashlights." He stood up, took one of the tapers from the candelabra and walked toward the hallway.

"Is there a generator?" John asked.

"No," Fred answered.

We sat looking at one another for a few minutes until Bruce came into the room with a box of stubby emergency candles and several boxes of matches walking through the dark since he evidently could find his way without illumination. The beam of a flashlight followed, and Eleanor carried in candlesticks and small saucers.

"I couldn't get to the other candlesticks," she said to Hextilda.

We watched, fascinated, as candles were lit, the wax dripped onto the saucers and then placed into the hardening surface.

"I believe our dinner is at an end, but I have one last question. Eleanor, do you know who tampered with my cookies?"

"In what way?" She looked down at the intact folded wafers and peered into the bowl, expecting to see something. "They look just as you left them," she said. "Except they were covered with a linen cloth." She turned to go back to the kitchen.

"Is there heat?" Julia asked.

"The boiler is fed by coal, so we may be fumbling around in the dark, but no one will freeze to death."

"Shouldn't you call someone?" Julia persisted.

"I don't think the telephone will be working," Fred answered as he helped Bruce make up additional lights for everyone. "We lost electricity once during a summer thunderstorm. I imagine the weight of the snow may have downed some of the lines."

"Maybe the power is out all over the area," John commented.

"Could be," Fred said.

"How can you be so casual about this," Joan said. "We could be stuck here for days! And no way of contacting anybody."

"Who were you hoping to chat with, dear?" Hextilda asked.

Allan returned with a flashlight in hand and Joan appealed to him. "The nanny. The girls were expecting us back by tomorrow night. Perhaps we can still make it."

Allan sighed. "The girls are old enough not to mind that we are there or not. The nanny will get them off to school Monday morning if we are not home by then. We don't have any alternative unless you want to hike out in what looks like three feet of snow."

Joan covered her mouth with her hand.

"Don't worry," I felt compelled to say. "We're all in the same boat of people expecting us to be somewhere Monday morning. Who knows, maybe the snow will melt by then."

John raised his eyebrows at me, and I realized it had been an overly optimistic thing to say.

"It's late. We may as well go to bed." Hextilda stood up and took one of the more elaborate candlesticks and made her way through the archway into the hall.

"Where is she going?" I asked Fred.

"Her bedroom is in the other wing above her study. She's weathered worse than this, I can assure you. We not only have heat and water but there's also a wood stove in the kitchen, so we'll be warm, clean and well-fed."

"If we run out of food, we'll draw lots to see who gets eaten first," Kent said, smiling.

"That's not in the least bit funny," Joan said, getting up abruptly, then taking the flashlight from Allan's hand and making her way out to the stairwell and stomping up the stairs.

"It wasn't," John said. "She's a mother and worried about her children. She'd like to reassure them that everything is all right. Just as I'm sure you'd like to call your school and let them know you might not be there on Monday."

Kent fumbled with his napkin and put it on the table. "Yes, you're right. Sorry." He took a saucer and candle and looked at José, his roommate for the night. "Are you coming up now?"

"I don't think so. I'll go to the library and choose something to read. Caroline?"

"Why don't we all go to the library?"

It seemed a reasonable thing to do rather than climb into bed so, with our little parade of lights, most of us followed her into the library, leaving Kent to help his sister negotiate the walk with the crutches while John and I brought up the rear in the event there was some trouble with her foot. It was slow going over the unfamiliar floor with intermittent carpeting and the flashlight's beam bobbing up and down.

As we approached the library, we could hear Caroline's voice.

"It is ridiculous that she should be in this enormous house by herself when we still have the house in Boston." There was the clicking sound of a lighter and a pause when she exhaled the first puff. "Look at the cost of the upkeep!"

"You seem to be happy enough to enjoy coming here, however," Fred commented calmly.

"I agree with Caroline entirely. The only reason she is holed up here so late in the season is to finish that blasted book. I have seen the sales reports and she isn't making the kind of money she used to. Well, none of us are, come to think of it. The point is, she would be more comfortable in Boston year-round where we could keep an eye on her," Allan said.

"Since when do you keep an eye on her?" Caroline asked.

"I have dinner with her every Wednesday and the girls stop by and see her from time to time. That's more than you do."

"I can hardly pop up for dinner once a week from Manhattan."

They were quiet for a few moments as we slowly progressed closer.

"I can't see why you're bothering with an art gallery, now of all times. Who is buying art in this economy?"

We reached the doorway and three heads swiveled in our direction.

"I'm guessing you heard some of our conversations."

"Complaining, you mean," Fred said.

"All right. Complaining. I admit it. Business is suffering, I am scraping to pay the tuition for the girls' schooling and here we sit in a monstrosity of a house that occupies half the county as it eats through what is left of our father's money." Allan sat down abruptly.

"It's Mother's money, not Father's anymore. And it's not ours, either."

Allan shot his brother a glance and, if looks could speak, they surely would have said, *Not yet.*

In retrospect, I don't know why we dragged Julia to the library just to hear a family of entitled strangers arguing about money, and it made for an uncomfortable encounter. Allan offered glasses of whiskey to us and, in an attempt to turn the conversation around, John began to ask him about grouse hunting, of all things. First, I had no idea that John hunted or if he had a gun of any sort but he had grown up out West, so it was likely that he knew enough to throw around terms relating to where the birds nested when the season opened and so forth.

I knew something about fine arts, having visited museums in New York many times, and so decided to have Caroline tell me about her art gallery. It became obvious that I was entirely ignorant of the sort of art that she displayed, was unfamiliar with the various movements or trends, and did not recognize any of the artists' names that she mentioned. She had a curious way of referring to a work of art as 'An Anderson,' for example, rather than saying it was a painting by So-and-so Anderson, implying that everyone should know who that was and what sort of work he did. I had to feel sorry for anyone who made their living creating and hoping to sell what they made since fashions of all sorts came and went.

Caroline stopped abruptly, aware that I did not recognize the people she mentioned and then sighed mightily. "I may have to close down the gallery anyway. Since the Crash, a lot of the artists have left the City—they simply can't afford it. I had a special group of customers who were just starting to collect and now they probably can't afford it either."

I didn't know how to respond but José took her hand. "You know there is one very good solution to your predicament." They smiled at each other, and I guessed he had asked her to marry him before and perhaps this was an honorable escape from her money troubles. I was embarrassed to be a witness to this private conversation, but José laughed at my discomfort.

"I have to bring this up in front of other people. It is the only way to paint her into a corner!"

"We'll talk after Christmas," she said.

"Actual Christmas or Ersatz Christmas? You know my family celebrates the feast of the Three Kings if you want to put off a discussion even further." He was teasing her.

"Soon, soon."

I couldn't see why she was so reluctant to commit herself except for a sense of pride in having her business succeed.

"If you want something to do, you could persuade Mother to give up Alistair and write something that people want to read, like travel guides," Allan suggested.

"Travel? Who can afford to travel now? And if you can, you probably would hire someone, not bring along a book."

"What about a humor book?"

"Jokes?" She looked at her brother as if he were out of his mind. "Mother can play pranks and jokes on us, but she can't take one." She pulled another cigarette out of a silver box on the table and José lit it with her lighter.

Did Caroline put the nasty quote in Hextilda's cookie? It would have been easy enough for her to do so, but why?

Chapter Fourteen

Between the whiskey before dinner, the wine with it and the nightcap, I was getting very sleepy and wanted very much to go to bed but felt responsible for Julia and how she would manage to get upstairs. I tried to stifle a yawn but was not successful and Allan looked at me.

"I can help Julia up the stairs," he said. "She's got the crutches, after all, and going up is safer than coming down."

I looked to John, and he shrugged his shoulders. "Go ahead up, we'll take care of her," he said.

The fire in the Great Room had been partially banked for the night and my thoughts returned to the two young women, Mariah and Nancy, who were at our beck and call from early morning and likely in the kitchen even now cleaning up from the meal.

Before I got ready for bed, I looked out the window, but it was so dark, I couldn't make out any landmarks; however, flakes were still beating against the windowpane. I undressed hastily and left the candle burning on the vanity for Julia's return, which woke me up when the door banged open.

"Sorry," Allan said, holding it open for her until she made her way to the other bed in the room. He nodded and shut the door.

"Do you need to use the washroom?" I asked, not looking forward to getting up to assist her.

"All done already. Everyone has been so kind," she added.

"Let me help you get the sock over your ankle," I said.

"I think I'll sleep with them on. I get the feeling it might be chilly. Otherwise, I can manage to get into the nightgown myself."

"Are you in any pain?" I asked. Aside from making grimaces when moving awkwardly, she didn't appear to be experiencing any great discomfort.

"This isn't the first time I've twisted that ankle. I think once you do, it is always susceptible to overextending. Anyway, I had a nip of the medicine, washed down with whiskey, so I should be good for the night."

I should think so, I thought. We had learned in our training that it was not a good idea to mix opiates with alcohol. I turned away while she undressed, and the house, previously quiet, came alive with a loud argument. I looked back to a wide-eyed Julia who seemed mesmerized by the racket.

"They're a volatile bunch," I said, feeling smug having been there one day more than she.

It was Allan and Joan in full voice and impossible not to hear the gist of the argument, which was that he paid attention to any woman other than his wife. There was some name-calling, loud enough that we could make out the words, 'liar' and 'fantasist,' rather polite considering the rude words people often used under the circumstances. It was remarkable that we could hear them since their room was on the other side of the gallery, but their voices seemed to echo off the ceiling of the Great Room and bounce over in our direction.

Julia turned to look me fully in the face. "I hope his helping me upstairs didn't cause all this commotion."

"Who knows? Everyone has been pulled in all directions emotionally and we've all had too much to drink. Trapped inside all day didn't help. I suggest we pretend we didn't hear anything and, like all polite guests, not remark on it tomorrow."

"I've had enough of this nonsense," Allan said. A door slammed and heavy footsteps came in our direction before he continued down the hall and pounded on someone's door. My curiosity got the better of me and I tiptoed to our door and opened it a crack to see where he was.

"I say, old man, would you mind if I bunked with you tonight?"

Poor John was the lucky recipient of a roommate—how could he say no? I closed the door and shook my head at the continuing drama. There was brief murmuring as they got settled, and before getting into bed, I asked Julia if she were ready, and then I went to the vanity to douse the candle for the night.

* * *

I awoke to a glaringly bright morning and assumed it must be late but picking up my wristwatch from the night table saw it was only seven-thirty. I got up and looked out the window to a clear sky, the sun above the horizon somewhere but obscured by the hills surrounding the valley along with the previous day's blizzard. Feeling like a child waking up to a snowy Christmas morning, I must have gasped at the sight of a nearly blinding snowfield.

"What is it?" Julia's worried voice asked.

"I'm sorry to have awakened you. I couldn't have imagined this much snow—I can't make out anything on the ground except the huge expanse of white."

She struggled out of bed, and I moved to help her, but she insisted on hopping on her good foot while holding on to the furniture. We stood looking down on what had been gravel and a lawn and through the glare, I could make out some trees in the distance.

"It's incredible," she said.

"Just imagine if you and Kent had been fully caught in that storm yesterday."

"We could have frozen to death," she said softly. "Oh, it's horrible to even think about."

I got the crutches from the corner of the room and followed her to the large washroom where we could both get ready for the day and then back to our room where she could at least change out of the dreadful sweater and jumper of the day before into a black turtleneck and wide-legged pants. I took the liberty of taking the sock off the injured ankle and unwinding the ACE bandage; I was surprised to see that it was not very swollen or bruised, which didn't mean it wasn't painful since she winced when I pressed gently on it.

"We'll have Doctor Taylor look at it in a bit. I don't know about you, but I am very hungry."

We made our way down to the warmth of the Great Room with its blazing fire, the result of someone's getting up early and feeding it huge logs, and then to the dining room where plates were laid out on the table and food was in chafing dishes on the sideboard.

"I guess we're the first ones up," Julia said. She craned her head to look at the doorway.

"Here, I'll fill your plate," I said, imagining the mess of trying to maneuver with crutches. "Eggs? Bacon? I believe these might be kippers." I turned up my nose at the oily fish displayed on an ornate china platter. "Coffee or tea?"

Settled a few minutes later with my plate, I savored the deep yellow scrambled eggs that spoke of chickens with a rich diet. While I ate enthusiastically, Julia pushed the food around on her plate with her eyes on the doorway.

"Did you sleep well?" I asked for something to say.

"Yes, well enough. It was very quiet all night."

"Compared to earlier, yes, it was." I smiled but she did not reciprocate.

"Mr. Mowbray got us in here yesterday—I don't know how on that winding road—but I'm wondering if he can get us out."

"I couldn't say. The snow looks very deep. I'm not familiar with this area but I wonder if the main road gets plowed."

"Oh, dear. I don't want to stay here."

I was surprised by her outburst and patted her hand, just as Miss Manley would have done under the circumstances. "We're not here forever, you know."

She tried to cover her anxiety with a small laugh. "It's just that I have to be back at work."

"I don't think you'll be back working tomorrow if that's what you had in mind. And can you work with your ankle like that?"

"I suppose so. I'm a secretary at an insurance company." She mentioned the name, one of the best known in New York.

"Since we're cut off from communication, who knows? Perhaps this storm made its way down to the City and many folks won't be able to get into work anyway."

I had run out of platitudes and reassurances and was hungry enough to return to the sideboard and try one of the fish, which turned out to be quite tasty, as were the scones and muffins that Eleanor must have made.

A noise in the hallway caught our attention and John came in, all smiles and good health.

"Good morning, lovely ladies," he said. He rubbed his hands together and looked over the spread on the sideboard.

"I trust you slept well?"

"I was going to ask the same of you," I said, looking up at him with a smile.

"Oh, yes. After a bit of noise just as I was settling down, things were fine. Actually, I slept like someone had hit me over the head! But here we are. Poor Allan must have been tuckered out by all the excitement. He's still fast asleep. Say, are these kippers? Haven't seen these in a long time." He sat down next to me, I poured him coffee and we began the discussion of the weather, the roads, the possibility of getting out, and so on until Fred came in and we four rehashed the same ground.

Normally, I would be done with breakfast and on with the business of the day but there was nothing to attend to, so we continued sitting, nibbling on the muffins, drinking coffee as one by one Hextilda, Adele, Caroline, José and Kent joined us, surprised at our early rising. At last, Allan entered, looking sheepish in his evening clothes of the night before.

"Why are you dressed like that?" his mother asked.

"Joan and I had a disagreement last night," he said.

"Allan, no need to expound. We all heard the commotion," Caroline said. She was looking at the breakfast offerings with disdain and decided to have only coffee.

"Well?" Hextilda asked as she looked her son over from head to toe. She expected him to change his clothes.

"I'm embarrassed to say she's locked me out. I've knocked on the door and she won't let me in."

Hextilda sighed. "I, for one, am going to have my breakfast in peace before we deal with Joan's tantrum. Allan nodded and we ate in peace before the topics of the weather, the road out, the lack of electricity and the telephone took over once again.

"I'd like to call Miss Manley to tell her we won't be back just yet."

"West Adams is not that far away. I'm sure people there know about this storm and probably are digging out themselves," John said.

"True. Whatever patients had appointments might not be able to show up anyway on Monday."

"Let's enjoy our holiday and be thankful that Mrs. Browne has the provisions to maintain us all and a cook to make the best of it."

"You don't think I'll let you sit idly in the library playing chess with Frederick all day, do you? There's shoveling to be done to get to the garages and check on the chickens, those lovely birds that have continued to lay so late in the season."

"Any cows to milk?" John asked with a smile.

"Lucky for you, no. Or I would have got you up at the crack of dawn when they needed to be milked."

We chatted while Mariah and Nancy came in to refill the coffee urn and the cream and remove the used plates and Eleanor appeared to ask if anything else was required. Hextilda asked if she had a key to

Allan and Joan's room and the woman didn't miss a beat and said she would find it.

"Please get her up, it's getting late. I'd have Allan do it, but we've had enough drama for a while."

It was about ten minutes later, as some of us were getting up from the table that Eleanor reappeared looking distressed, or I should say, showing more emotion than I had seen so far.

"Ma'am. Something dreadful has happened."

Hextilda stood up suddenly, as did Allan and they both followed Eleanor out of the room, up the nearby staircase, following the trajectory of the gallery around to the open door of what must have been Allan and Joan's room. The rest of us were not far behind, except for Julia and Kent who had migrated into the Great Room to watch the proceedings from below.

"Oh, my God!" Hextilda exclaimed in the doorway before Allan pushed her out of the way and yelled out his wife's name.

John and Fred went the remaining way swiftly, with Caroline and me in tow, until we were all crowded outside the door, trying to look into the large room. The windows were wide open to the cold wind that blew across the snow outside and made it nearly freezing in the room. I stood on tiptoe to get a better view. In the middle of the bed, Joan lay on her back, a peaceful look on her face and the sgian-dubh sticking out of her chest.

Chapter Fifteen

A moment of silence was followed by a babble of voices expressing horror, shock and some practical suggestions.

"How could this happen? She locked me out!" Allan said.

"Who else has a key to this room?" Caroline asked

"What will I tell the girls?" Allan moaned.

"Please, step aside so we can take a closer look," Fred said. "Why are those blasted windows wide open?"

John walked over and carefully pulled the sashes down which stopped the wind, but the temperature was unbearably cold. He put his hand on the radiator and said, "Someone shut off the radiator, too."

"Why?" Hextilda asked.

"So we would have difficulty determining the time of death."

"Is she dead?" Caroline, whose view was blocked, asked in a whisper.

"Yes, you idiot," Allan growled.

"It was a ritual murder," Hextilda proclaimed, and everyone

looked at her. "I told you someone was out to get me, but they were trying to put an end to the entire Comyn line."

"Mother, do shut up about that nonsense," Allan yelled, pushing himself fully into the room and glaring at us standing in the doorway.

She did and sat down on a chair in the hallway with her hands folded in her lap looking calm. Caroline came to stand beside her, followed by José who put his arm around her shoulders.

I was the only one left outside the door and John beckoned me in.

"Could you get a towel or cloth?"

There was a small sink in the room like the one in mine and hand towels hung from bars on either side. I brought one to him and he asked Allan to step back and turn away while he carefully pulled out the dagger trying to preserve what fingerprints there might be.

He covered her with the sheet, but Allan put his hand on his arm.

"I need to see her face again."

It was poignant to hear, then heartbreaking to see him kiss her forehead and put the sheet back up. Fred was watching his brother carefully for signs of shock, and Allan did stumble a bit before sitting down heavily on a chair and loosening his tie. I eased myself out of the room and checked that Hextilda was being tended by her daughter before going down to the Great Room, pouring myself a half glass of whiskey and taking a gulp while Kent and Julia stared at me.

"What's going on?" he asked.

"I'm afraid Joan has died."

Julia cried out, "Oh, no!" and Kent put his arm around her.

I could tell they wanted to ask further questions but there was no way I was going supply the details. I took the glass and went to the library just to be by myself. This entire weekend had been surreal, with Hextilda's weird machinations and manipulations, the dynamic of the family, the storm and that damned dagger. I was sure someone was going to suggest that she killed herself which, judging by the precise placement of the knife, would have been impossible. She had probably been asleep, lying on her back when someone came in and attacked her. But why?

It was obvious she and her husband sniped at each other and had a loud quarrel last night, but kill his wife? Hextilda had been relentless in her digs at Joan and the bairn in the Dundee cake was mean-spirited, but if she was so concerned about continuing the Comyn male line, then killing the only person who could legitimately give birth to that descendant was counterproductive. On further thinking, Fred could provide an heir, if he were married and had children, which he could certainly do. From everything John had said about him, it seemed highly unlikely that he was in such a rivalry with his older brother that he would stoop to killing Joan.

The thoughts rolled around in my head. Bruce and Eleanor? But what stake did they have in this family? Caroline and José? Who was José anyway? He passed himself off as the wealthy son of some Latin American ambassador with his suave ways and attentiveness to his girlfriend, but he seemed careful to reveal little of himself aside from that glittering smile and smooth manners. Julia and Kent were another interesting pair, appearing out of nowhere in the middle of a snowstorm, both seemingly normal people although Kent's being a teacher was far-fetched unless schools were scraping the bottom of the barrel.

I tossed the rest of the whiskey down and thought it was a heck of a way to start a Sunday. I wished I were back in West Adams, accompanying Miss Manley to church and having a simple roast for dinner instead of these pompous exhibitions of excess that the Brownes enjoyed.

"There you are," John said from the doorway. He sat beside me and kissed me on the cheek. "Was it too much for you?"

"No," I scoffed. "This place and these people are too much for me. Seeing Joan like that was appalling and the family's bizarre reactions...."

"I know. As one of the only disinterested persons here, I took the dagger into my possession and tucked it into a safe place. Who knows what evidence the police can get from it."

"What about her body?"

"This sounds a bit macabre, but they've decided to put her down in the basement for now. Fred said it is cold down there, undisturbed for the most part and can be locked."

I exhaled. "The dungeon. How awful."

"Let's go back to the others. We need to talk about a way forward."

I dreaded going to the Great Room and seeing Allan, who now looked more puzzled and confused than shocked and sad. Fred seemed to have taken the lead in the discussion of what to do next and had assembled the entire household, the Mowbrays and the two young helpers included, into the room.

He began very calmly. "Some of you know that Joan died during the night and, when the telephone is working again, the authorities will be notified. But there might be a way to get some assistance before that."

"Kent, Julia, since this is a family matter, may I request that you leave the room so we can discuss the next steps in private," Hextilda said.

They were startled but nodded and made their way toward the archway leading to the hall and I guessed on to the sitting room so that Julia didn't have to tackle the stairs. Hextilda looked over at her staff, including Adele, and nodded, indicating that they could also leave. I looked over at John and wondered why she hadn't asked us or José to go, but she took command of the situation.

"This is what I think. You know that the Comyn name has been a great birthright and also a curse. Back in the days of...."

"Mother, please. This is no time for days of yore," Caroline said.

"Hear me out. Somebody in this house would like to see the end of the Comyn clan and I believe that is why Joan was killed." She lowered her voice. "What do we know of this Kent and Julia? Perhaps they are part of the great opposition. They just happened to be hiking nearby? That beggars belief. What about Bruce and Eleanor?"

"Oh, come on, Mother. That is ridiculous."

"The Mowbrays were once supporters of our family but there is always envy in a Scotsman's heart. Mark my words, they've worked for us for years but there is a strain of hostility under the skin with those two."

Everyone was quiet, not knowing how to deal with her theory.

"Well, Eleanor did have a key to the room," Allan said.

"I'm sure many keys are floating around. Do you believe there is some tribal grudge that they have been harboring for years? And suddenly, apropos of nothing, they decide to strike out against Allan's wife?" Fred asked.

By the jut of her jaw, Hextilda was not backing down. "Think what you like, but I know human motivations, having written about them for years. Now, I am going to my study and Adele and I are going to work on the final chapters." To everyone's surprise, she got up and went back to work on her latest opus.

"She has lost her marbles," Allan said to us all. "She is barking mad! Who knows or cares about the Comyn clan except her?"

Caroline shook her head in dismay. "She has been acting odd lately."

"She never liked Joan," Allan said. "She didn't hold back on her remarks to Joan when we had two daughters and no sons. We were perfectly happy with them—we don't need a son to make things better. What if her mania about an heir to the clan led her to kill Joan?"

Chapter Sixteen

John, Fred, Allan and Bruce had the sad task of taking Joan's body out of the room on a makeshift stretcher and for a horrible moment I thought they might bring it through the Great Room on their way to the basement. However, they used the stairway on the other side and walked solemnly down and out of our view. It was some time before they returned and by that time, I was the only one left sitting by the large fire, wondering what we should all do next.

That question was answered when John came back by himself and sat beside me.

"We've decided that we ought to go out to the main road and see if we can get a ride from someone into Stamford."

I was dumbfounded. "We?"

"Fred and I. None of the cars could make it but we could cross-country ski up there."

"The drive to the main road is winding and uphill. And then through the woods. How do you propose to find your way with every-thing covered in several feet in snow?"

"Fred knows the way."

"You can't do this! It sounds dangerous and foolhardy and...."

"What do you suggest instead?"

"Most obviously, stay here until the electricity and phone come back on. Or the snow melts a bit so you can see the road. Surely Bruce's vehicle can get out—he got in here with those two."

John looked down at his hands.

"Well, I'm going with you!" I said, standing up.

"Do you know how to cross-country ski?" he asked.

"Of course not. I don't know how to downhill ski, either. But I'm not going to stay here while you two gallivant across the fields and hills, falling into ditches, crashing into trees, or getting buried by an avalanche."

"I think it would be safer for you to stay here."

"Are we each supposed to go to our rooms and lock the door, like in every mystery book? Especially since I couldn't lock my room from the inside although someone has access to keys. Or are we all supposed to stay in one room, glaring at each other with suspicion until someone breaks?"

"I also thought you would be the perfect person to...."

"Hold down the fort?"

"Well, you are so reliable."

"I hate that people peg me as 'reliable.' Good old reliable Aggie. Well, I can be as dramatic and as angry as anyone else." At that, I stamped my foot on the floor.

He paused a moment and looked down to hide a smile. "Yes, I can see."

"Don't you laugh at me!" I said, near to tears after the events of the morning and the thought of the danger he was putting himself in.

He took my hands in his and looked up at me. "Darling, may I call you darling?"

"You may but not if the intent is to further persuade me that what you are doing is sensible. Because it is not."

He pulled me back down onto the loveseat. "We plan to leave

shortly, which will give us plenty of time to get out to the main road, see if it is passable and flag someone down. We intend to pass a message along to the police and be back here before dark."

"It will be dark sometime after four o'clock," I said looking at my watch to gauge how long it would take them to complete their mission.

"It's uphill going out but downhill coming back, remember?"

I said nothing, just looked at my hands in his.

"All right, you'd better get a move on."

He kissed me lightly and got up to change into suitable outdoor clothing.

This was going to be an awful day of waiting, with scenes of catastrophe dogging my brain the entire time he was gone. It made me think of my poor mother when my father was in France during the Great War. How did she get through every day without thoughts of danger, disaster and disease? I remember she was a bundle of nerves, waiting for a letter each day and re-reading it to detect whether my father was trying to keep any information from her. Some days there was not a letter and then two came the following day and she practically wept with relief knowing all was well.

Until it wasn't and he got gassed.

Reliability must run in the Burnside family because even in that state in the hospital, he kept up a constant correspondence home so my mother wouldn't worry too much. She had such relief to know that he was coming home, and Eddie and I caught the contagion of her happiness, which was dampened when she met him at the train station and saw how ill he was. He was so thin and weak that he couldn't even pick up Eddie and coughed every time he tried to speak. It took many months for him to recover to the point of being physically functional and the emotional toll on all of us was extreme.

Thinking of all that happened when I was a little girl and that life seemed precarious made me appreciate how tough my parents were, but it also highlighted that danger could happen at any moment and events were so often out of our control. War, disease and death were some that we couldn't see coming and neither was murder, for surely what happened to Joan was murder and that person was still in the house with us. Hopefully not intending to strike again.

* * *

I was right on two accounts: the cross-country ski endeavor looked as foolhardy as I imagined when I watched the two men bumble across the yard, digging their poles into the deep snow and trying to get into the rhythm of forward motion. The other thing I was right about is that it was a very long day. Caroline and José stayed mostly in the library, coming out periodically to announce that the telephone was still not working. Kent and Julia stayed together in one of the other rooms, perhaps trying to be sensitive to the family tragedy or just feeling in the way. Allan had disappeared from view entirely and I hoped he wasn't keeping vigil in the basement—an image too sad to entertain. The Mowbrays and their young assistants came and went, tidying the bedrooms, picking up used glasses, emptying ashtrays, offering tea to whoever wished it. Hextilda and Adele were off in the author's study creating another obstacle for Alistair to overcome, and that gave me the idea to continue reading her novel—a distraction I badly needed.

I brought her book from my room and went to the library and, out of curiosity or a need to poke holes in Hextilda's wild accusations, searched the bookcases for something about the Comyn clan. Naturally, there was an entire shelf devoted to the clans of Scotland and I took down several and sat at the table and began to read about the events that may have shaped the current conflict in her mind.

The first book had such an extraordinarily long introduction written in flowery prose about the prestigious family and how ill-treated they had been over time that made me look back to see the author's name. It wasn't Comyn. But the more I read, it became obvious that the wealthy and landed families intermarried so frequently that everyone seemed to be related to everyone else.

Putting the book down for a moment I had the realization about the origins of the fairy tales where the poor girl meets her prince. Of course, they were fairy tales; there was no chance that someone with significant land and money would marry anyone who hadn't the same to enter into a bargain, which is what marriage was in those days.

I looked up and noticed for the first time an enormous genealogical tree in a frame hung above one bookcase, a man and woman in prayer on either side of what must be the Comyn trunk with branches extending through numerous generations identified by a small scroll with a name in Latin. The print was too small to be able to decipher even if I could read Latin, which I could not, and it made me wonder who got included in this depiction of the family and who was left out. Were these the male and female offspring or just the men from each generation? Surely there must have been many more names to include, which made me think these were the oldest sons or in the event of lack of sons, the nephews or cousins. The script was so tiny that the uppermost names were illegible from where I stood so I had no idea when the tree was compiled and with whom it ended.

I replaced the book I had been looking at on the shelf and found a more modern volume that was about the clans in general and the political and military jigsaw that evolved as families jostled for land, money and power. The earliest identifiable Comyn, Richard, had a son who married a woman named Hextilda—aha! That's where that extraordinary name originated and until the present generation likely never appeared again. Both families were well connected and involved as advisors to the Scottish king and held castles and control of vital passes over the mountains.

Another Comyn was John "The Red", presumably for his hair color; it was about this time that English rulers inserted themselves into this complicated, multi-generational push and pull, making alliances and forcing alliances. His son, John "The Black", considered himself one of the potential claimants to the throne after the death of the incumbent. Based on the intricate dynastic ancestry, he was one of a handful. For reasons of preference, or perhaps the lack of a significant bribe, he was not chosen, and things seemed to be smooth for a while.

Then the chapter heading, "The Wars of Independence," referred to the numerous attempts to get out from under the English yoke and the prominent role of the Comyns in those battles before they pledged their loyalty to King Edward I, also known as Long-shanks and the Hammer of the Scots. Robert the Bruce, usually considered the hero of Scottish Independence, killed "The Red" in a church in Dumfries for murky reasons. Conveniently, the Comyn lands were forfeited to the crown and their prominence in Scottish politics and land ownership was severely reduced.

I had only got to the fourteenth century and not even halfway through the book and I skimmed over the remaining centuries of land grabs, clan conflicts and intermarriages to the end to see who was the current Laird of Cumming, as they subsequently spelled their name. Flipping back to the front I saw the publication date was forty years earlier, so I had no idea who it might be, but judging from what I had read and how long the Brownes had lived in the United States, there was a good chance that nobody in this branch of the family stood in proximity to that title. Even though I had not read the volume care-fully, there didn't appear to be any special dagger associated with the family. The business Hextilda tried to sell us on our first night about the truth-telling abilities of the knife I had considered hogwash from the beginning and now even more so. But why had she concocted that ridiculous story? Was she really only trying to reveal peoples' motivations? Or did she actually believe in some of the nonsense herself? You could never tell with authors.

A gong sounded and I realized it was time for a lunch that turned out to be more of a buffet than a served meal, understandably since the Mowbrays had plenty to do as it was. I hadn't seen the Mowbray name in the clan book, but I would return to the library and look again. Bruce—that was a common enough name, but was he related to The Bruce? I would ask Fred later.

The thought that Fred and John were not there to join us, as I faced two empty chairs, gave a nervous twist to my stomach but I didn't comment to anyone. We were subdued, Caroline and José talking to each other in low tones, Kent and Julia wary and quiet, and even Hextilda was silent for once.

"How far it is out to the main road?" I asked.

Caroline gave a small laugh. "As far as it was when you came in."

I know I turned red at what seemed a stupid question, but I plowed on. "I meant, how many miles is it?"

She seemed either not to know or not to care and shook her head.

"I think the family has never paid attention to such details," José said, whether supporting the stupidity of the question or mildly mocking their lack of observation.

"Far enough," came the reply from Eleanor, who had come in with a platter of fruit for dessert. She placed it on the sideboard and left without another word.

"I was just reading about the Comyn family in the library," I said to Hextilda. "What a fascinating history."

"It makes for good fiction except in their case it was reality. Constant warfare, rivalries, alliances, misalliances. It's a wonder anyone survived to produce so many descendants. Not many people use the Comyn name anymore. It's more liking Cumming or Cummings and all sorts of variations, but the same family."

She must have decided that was enough to say and continued eating while I, brought up to have a conversation at the table, thought I might ease everyone's nerves by continuing along with the family discussion.

"Kent, are you and Julia Scottish by any chance?"

They looked up as if I had slandered them, looked at each other and decisively in unison said, "No."

Realizing the tone of their response might be considered offensive, Julia amended her answer. "We're of French and English heritage. You?"

"The same, although our hostess originally thought I was a Burns, as in Robbie Burns, I suppose."

Again, the conversation died, and I decided to be quiet for the remainder of the meal as did everyone else.

"If you'll excuse me," I said. "I think I'll bundle up and take a stroll outside." I wasn't joking; I needed to get some fresh air but the lot of them looked at me as if I were insane.

I was anxious to see what the weather conditions were and if the snow was as impassible as it appeared from my view from the windows. I put on two layers of pants, knowing that each would likely be soaked through by the end of even a short walk, a turtleneck, a fisherman's sweater and thick socks and headed to the mudroom off the kitchen to retrieve my boots, coat and hat.

Eleanor and Bruce were seated at the table in the middle of the kitchen, not talking but they still looked at me with apprehension as if they had been overheard.

"Are you going out?" Bruce asked.

"Yes, I'm just going to walk a bit."

"Don't go out of sight of the house. I'm not rescuing anybody else."

"If the snow gets too deep, I'll turn back. I just wanted to see how difficult it might be for Fred and John to make their way to the road."

"Don't you try going up the road. You won't be able to find it anyway."

"As I said, I'm just going to walk a bit."

I went into the mudroom, annoyed by their lack of compassion or interest. A few minutes later, twice my normal bulk, I waddled through the door into the crisp early afternoon. There was practically no wind, and it was soothingly quiet in a way the oppressive silence of indoors was not. I stood for a few minutes just inhaling the air, imagining that West Adams might be experiencing some of this early winter weather and wondering if Miss Manley was stuck inside or if one of the neighbors had dug a path out. The area immediately outside the kitchen had been shoveled down to the gravel, as was a path to the garages, and I made my way there rather than try my way through the high drifts. The snow crunched beneath my boots, and I looked to see that the cars had been parked quite a distance from the house and poor Bruce must have been the one to have shoveled that path. If that's why he was grumpy, I could certainly understand.

There was a side door to the garage and stepping over the threshold I was surprised to see room for even more than the six cars that had been parked there as well as a workshop or repair area toward the back. I went to turn on the light, but the click produced nothing, of course, and there was probably nothing worth seeing beyond the spare tires hanging on the wall and a set of jumper cables. Wait—John said there weren't any. Or did he say no one could help him start his car? Or had he just been dismissive of my wanting to return home?

Puzzled and annoyed, I walked back toward the kitchen and then decided to circumnavigate the house, staying within a few feet of the actual structure where I assumed the ground was level. It was slow going, with me having to lift a leg very high to plant in the snow for each step. I must have looked ridiculous and started to giggle but it was a nice bit of exercise even though I made up my mind to go to the corner and retrace my steps, an easier method of walking than trudging onward through the deep snow.

The last bit of my walk took me toward the library, and I could see Hextilda and Allan in an animated conversation through the windows. It was incredible that even through those thick windows I could hear that it was not a pleasant tone between them but one of accusation and recrimination. At one point Allan took some papers off the table and waved them around as if to make some point but his mother's mouth was clamped shut as if in disagreement or defiance.

I moved backward quickly, certain that they hadn't seen me in the midst of whatever argument they were engaged in. Then, finding my former footsteps in the snow, I high-stepped back to the back door, being sure to stamp the snow off my boots before entering.

I suddenly felt incredibly hot dressed in so many layers entering the warm house, so I took off my outer clothes, removed my boots and walked through the now empty kitchen in my stocking feet and up to my room. I changed my clothes and thought to read, then remembered that I had left my book in the library. Well, I would just have to retrieve it and hope that the Brownes were done with whatever disagreement they were involved in.

To my relief the library proved empty and I decided to join Alistair in his latest escapade, which was merely an escape from my wondering and worrying when Fred and John would get back. The day wore on, as did the adventures in the Highlands, and the light began to fade outside. This was what I had most feared, that they would not return before nightfall, or they would get lost in the snow. And suppose they had managed to get a lift to town? Good for them, mission accomplished, but there would be no sense in trying to return in the dark and no way for them to let us know that they had made it safely.

Or not.

Daylight was gone and then I wondered if either of them had thought to bring a flashlight. Or food. Or water. I was a bundle of nerves listening for any sound, but the house was a quiet as a tomb. And yes, I reminded myself, it was a tomb.

Finally, at the far end of the house near the kitchen, I thought, I could hear noise and I ran past the dinner preparations in the kitchen to see Fred at the back door stacking his skis against the wall.

"Where's John?" Fred and I said simultaneously.

"We were together all the way up to the road and managed to wave down a farmer with a horse and cart to whom we gave a message. Then we turned around and went carefully until we got to the drive down to the house."

"And then?"

"We were joking around a bit about skiing and the next thing I knew he had taken off downhill."

I waited for the rest—fell into a ditch, hit a tree, smashed into a boulder.

"He disappeared out of view. You know how the path winds as

you come down into the valley so you can't see where it will take you. And it was getting dark by then."

"How could he follow the road when you said you couldn't see it for all the snow?"

"I have an idea how it lays. But he didn't. He simply took off and I assumed he'd gotten back here well before me."

Chapter Seventeen

"Now what?" I asked. I was worried and angry at both of them, Fred for suggesting this harebrained excursion, John for participating in it as if it were an adventure and then his absurd action of careening down the hill in the near dark. I must have raised my voice because the clatter in the kitchen ceased, and I felt I had to explain myself.

"Doctor Taylor didn't come back. I'm afraid he might be lost."

Bruce appeared with his long-suffering look, imagining a long night out looking for the foolish man, and he walked deliberately to the mudroom, sat down and began to lace up his boots in no hurry.

"Did you happen to take flashlights with you?" I asked and Fred's sheepish look gave the answer I didn't want to hear.

"Have something to eat before you go," Eleanor said to her husband.

My shoulders dropped in dismay. Everybody was taking their time and John was out there—somewhere—perhaps with a broken leg. Or frostbite. I was trying to keep my nerves at bay, but I could feel the dread creeping up from my knees into my gut.

The chatter in the kitchen picked up between the two young girls and Eleanor asked Bruce what else she could get him. I could have screamed with impatience.

There was a crash and I thought Fred's skis had clattered to the floor, but when entering the mudroom, I was shocked to see John there, his skis still on his feet, standing half in and half out of the door.

Fred laughed and clapped him on the shoulder, and I gave a stony look.

"You know that thing where you stamp your foot? I think it would be totally in line if you did that right about now," John said.

"Since you are ambulatory and seemingly in charge of your senses, I will leave you to your ski pal while I go up and change for dinner." I turned on my heel and walked through the kitchen, my head held high as I heard the chuckling behind me.

Dinner was to be another dress-up affair and I put on the red frock that I had worn the first night. I was not going to go down early and listen to John's apologies, if he had even thought about how worried I had been. I guessed he would have a story to dine out on for some time to come, a bit at my expense.

There was a knock on my door, and I opened it to his apologetic face.

"I am very sorry if I frightened you, Aggie. It was certainly not intentional. I thought I would try a bit of downhill skiing and suddenly I whooshed down the hill going very fast and ended up going quite far until I rolled over a few times."

"Are you hurt?" He had my sympathy at last.

"A bit bruised, that's all. When I brushed myself off and got up, I must have lost my bearings and thought I was headed straight for the house but ended up in that patch of woods that we walked through with Fred. I recognized where I was at last and made a directional adjustment, trudged on and finally saw the lights from the house."

"That was very lucky on your part, considering there is no moon out."

"Are you going down already?" he asked, looking at his watch.

"It's early. I thought I would have time for a quick bath before dinner."

"Go ahead, and I'll explain to everyone. They'll be dying to hear of your adventure."

I closed the door, shaking my head at what men do sometimes, and put on my pearls and some lipstick. With any luck, this might be the last night we had to stay here. Well, with lots of luck, I thought, since we were still operating by candlelight. It made me realize how dangerous it must have been before electricity, especially for women with their flowing skirts around fireplaces, candles and stoves. Thank goodness for flashlights, one of which I now possessed. Taking one last look around the room I wondered where Julia had decided to stay on the first floor rather than tackling the stairs with crutches.

It was eerie to look over the gallery railing into the Great Room where the fire cast its strange shapes onto the walls and the shadows of the weaponry made them appear that much larger and more menacing. Not for the first time I wondered why Hextilda kept the feudal and militaristic décor long after the death of her husband. Although he had been mentioned several times, I wondered about his personality, which had to have been as strong or stronger than his wife's, to keep up with her. Then again, some widows came into their own more fully once their spouse had died. Hextilda didn't strike me as one of them, however.

I was first down and took the liberty of pouring a small bit of whisky into a glass before Allan could appear and fill it nearly to the top; I felt I had been drinking too much since arriving. There was a bowl full of nuts that I decided would be too messy to tackle and instead waited for the hors d'oeuvres.

A figure appeared in the doorway, and I stood up to greet my hostess but saw that it was Adele, and I was once again struck by how similar they were in build.

"Please, don't get up. Is it just the two of us? How nice," she said. "We can have a pleasant chat before the fireworks begin." She smiled mischievously at me. "That calls for a drink, don't you think?"

She had been so quiet and in the background previously that it hadn't occurred to me that she had a pointed sense of humor.

"How long have you worked for Hextilda?" I asked as she sat next to me. She was probably in her early thirties, but the old-fashioned hairstyle and the whiff of lavender made her seem almost of another era.

"About four years. I came on when Mr. Browne was very ill. Despite what you might think is her steely exterior, she was very upset about his passing for some time afterward."

"I can imagine." I was silent, knowing that it was one of the ways to get someone else talking.

"The children—well, they're adults, after all—were devastated. I don't think they knew the state of his finances." She paused to take a sip of her drink. "I can't imagine how much it cost to purchase this land and build this enormous house, but I think everyone is worried about how they can maintain it into the future."

"They have a home in Boston, too, I understand."

"It is a very grand home, and I am lucky to be able to enjoy it. I fear one of the properties will have to be sold at some point to meet the expenses. After the Crash, nobody's finances have been in good shape."

Except for mine, I thought, because I was too young and new to the wide world to have done any investing.

"Even I, country mouse that I am, had put some money in stocks. Thank goodness, it wasn't much, and it certainly isn't much now. Well, I learned my lesson."

"I'm sorry to hear that."

"Hello, all," Fred said, entering the Great Room, the beam of his flashlight bobbing up and down as he walked. He clicked it off and stood looking into the fire a moment before turning to us. "How is Allan? I haven't seen him since I got back."

"I'm afraid I don't know," Adele said. "I've been holed up with your mother all day."

"Deadline, correct?"

She nodded.

"I do wish she would not push herself so hard. And probably you, too."

"That's the job," she smiled.

"I'm sure you would like to hear about our adventure today, but I'll wait until everyone is here so as not to repeat myself. What did you do today, Aggie, other than worry about what we were doing?"

"That was not foremost on my mind," I answered as if it were of no great importance. "I was deep in Scottish history in the library, looking up the Comyns."

"Aye," he said. "Pardon the very bad accent."

"The Red Comyn, The Black Comyn, what an extraordinary family they were."

"It's been a while since I revisited that history but as I remember they were a land-grabbing, power-hungry bunch."

Adele laughed. "I think you had to be then, or you would be left in the dust. Just look at what continues to happen to Alistair with all his noble intentions. He doesn't know where he gets his next bowl of porridge, even if your mother does."

"Now, now, Adele. It's why it's called fiction. Suspension of belief." It was Hextilda, so accustomed to her own home that she came in from the dark hallway and archway without a candle or flashlight, though she held onto the furniture as she made her way over to us.

"True. It's what people love about your hero. Without a penny to his name or a house to call his own for very long, he can get out of any difficulty, fight the evil English and win the fair maiden."

"Almost win her," Hextilda corrected. "They have the longest courtship in history. We'll see. Perhaps the next book will have a big wedding, fraught with obstacles getting to the altar, naturally."

"It would be a fitting end to the series," Fred said.

His mother looked at him without emotion. "Yes, it would. It might be time. But that's for next year. Pour me a whiskey, dear."

We chatted and heard the thump of Julia on her crutches, accompanied by Kent who held the flashlight. She was surprisingly agile as she put them to one side and hopped to the couch.

"Wouldn't you like to put your foot up?" Hextilda asked.

"No, thank you. It actually doesn't bother me that much. I may just ditch these sticks," she said. "I'll have Doctor Taylor give it a look tonight. As I said, I've turned it before."

Kent got her a whiskey and one for himself and shortly thereafter Allan and John walked across the gallery and joined us in the Great Room. Allan bent to kiss his mother on the cheek, and she smiled sadly at him.

"Well, tell us what went on today," Allan asked his brother.

"I don't know that I have ever walked out to the road from the house, but I can tell you that it is quite a climb, especially in skis. It took us several hours. We got a great workout. Once into the forest above, it was smooth sailing since the lack of trees showed us where the road lay, and we made it out to the main road safely enough. It had not been plowed so we stood for a while wondering if we should try to ski down to Stamford or up toward the nearest farm before realizing that could take too much time and the farm, though closer, wouldn't be of any use as they were as snowed in as we are and likely don't have a telephone on top of it. Then, out of nowhere, we heard this jingling and we looked at each other as if Kris Kringle had come early, only to see a man driving a horse and cart. The noise was the harness bells."

That got a chuckle out of the solemn group.

"We were not specific about our errand, only that we wanted to get word to the sheriff that we needed assistance and he said he could relay that message somehow. He was kind enough to ask if we wanted to stay with him as it would get dark soon and we gave it some thought and decided it was better to come back here and report on our progress."

"We went back through the woods, finding the path we had made fairly easily, and I can tell you, the light was starting to fade already, and I knew we had to hotfoot it back. And now, I think John needs to relate the exciting part of the journey."

John began a little sheepishly. "It's been a while since I've been downhill skiing and I don't know what I was thinking except that my legs were sore from our climb up and out and all I wanted to do was get back and stand by this warm fire. So, we came out of the woods and there is a little incline...."

"It's quite an incline," Fred added.

"Yes, as it turned out. I thought I would just go slowly down but I gathered speed and could almost see our tracks from the ascent."

"He was completely out of sight in a minute."

"And zooming faster than I thought possible. I must have gone quite a way at a tremendous speed before I hit a rock or something and went head over heels into the snow. It knocked the wind out of me and banged me about, but I got up expecting to see Fred coming down at any moment."

"What he didn't know was that he had veered off in the wrong direction and must have been heading away from the house."

"I wasn't going anywhere just then. I sat in the snow and checked that I hadn't done any great damage to myself or the skis, caught my breath and headed off in what turned out to be the wrong direction. It wasn't until I came upon the woods above the lake that I recognized where I was and, turning back, could faintly see the lights from the house."

"You were very lucky," Allan said.

"Yes, I know it. I bear the bruises from the fall and the crushing embarrassment of having got myself lost. I apologize to any and all of you for the worry I caused."

"Oh, stop it," Fred said. "Nobody cares about you except Aggie, and I don't know why she does." His comment made everyone laugh as the gong sounded for dinner.

Chapter Eighteen

A dele helped a wobbly Hextilda into the dining room, and I suspected she might have had a drink too many from a private decanter before joining us for a pre-dinner drink. She plopped down into her chair and exhaled loudly, then urged us to come in and eat.

"We've had misfortune before and we'll have it again, but we need to eat."

It seemed an insensitive thing to say—as if Joan's death was an accident, which it surely was not, or an inconvenience to the steady operation of the household.

"Mother, do be kind," Fred said.

She waved her hand in dismissal and John and I exchanged glances; I was sure he shared my thoughts that we were about to experience another disastrous family meal.

"Our mother? Be kind? Ha!" was Allan's comment. "You couldn't give Joan the time of day, the poor thing."

"Poor thing? She's the one with the money you gladly spend, and you never treated her very well despite it."

Allan's face had turned red, and he drank down the remainder of the whiskey in his glass.

Eleanor and her two assistants came in with a baked ham just as Hextilda nodded off to sleep in her chair. Everyone looked at everyone else wondering what to do but it was Caroline to the rescue.

She spoke in a whisper, "I think we are about to experience one of the more enjoyable meals in this house." We all stifled sniggers, including the servers, who held out the platter of sliced meat to us in turn, then the sweet potatoes, then the green beans and finally the freshly baked brown bread.

We heard from José at last about his education in the States and his desire to continue to live here after his father's assignment had concluded.

"Why is that?" Julia asked.

"Your newspapers don't print many stories about my country and certainly not our politics. There will be an election in January, and, likely, my father's party will no longer be in the majority and his appointment will be over. That's how it goes."

"That's terrible," Julia said.

"It's how it works everywhere," Fred said. "New president, new ambassadors. And lest I sound too cynical, those appointments usually come after a hefty campaign donation."

"True," Allan agreed.

José nodded in agreement, not at all hesitant to admit that his family had played the same game. He then gave us a rundown on neighboring Latin American countries, the political parties, the coalitions of military, Church and the old families that kept things 'in order,' as he put it.

"Gosh, I had no idea," Kent said.

Not for the first time did I wonder if he could possibly be a civics teacher and not possess knowledge of the broader world and how it worked. It made me a little bold.

"Tell me, Kent, what sort of civics curriculum is there at your school?"

He had just put a forkful of food into his mouth, buying him less than a minute to come up with a satisfactory answer but his sister jumped in instead.

"It's very rigorous. We both attended as students. That's partially how Kent got the job—they knew him already."

"And because he was a stellar student?" Caroline asked.

"I'll be the first to admit I was not top of my class, but that's not always the key to success, is it?"

"Not at all," Hextilda said, coming out of her stupor. "My late husband was nearly at the bottom of his class at Princeton and look at the tremendous success he had in life." She swung her arm out to indicate the luxurious setting and knocked over the glass of wine onto the table where it shattered.

"Oh, my. Better call Eleanor back in to clean this up," she said to no one in particular.

And that is who responded. No one. We sat looking at her, perhaps all of us wondering how she could have become such an awful person.

"Oh, Mother," Caroline said, taking her plate and gingerly picking up the pieces one by one. We watched in silence.

"Well, you may think that I am ill-behaved, but your father was the worst."

Oh, no, where is this going now? I thought.

She looked around the table to each of us in turn. "I began to write my books because he was never around. Too busy building his empire to pay attention to me or the children. Why do you think Alistair is such a wonderful creature? Handsome, daring, bold, accomplished in all the military arts, loving, lustful, all the things your father was not. He was jealous of a fictional man! Think of it!"

The dishes were cleared, and Eleanor brought in an apple pie with an elaborate crust that when cut wafted cinnamon into the air. The pieces served, the whipped cream passed around and she left without a word.

Hextilda seemed to wait for the footsteps to recede before to turning her attention to Allan. "After you were born, he thought we'd done such a bad job of creating a child that I got pregnant again. Hence, Frederick." She smiled at her second son. "And to get back at me for creating Alistair, he decided to seduce my assistant."

Everyone's head turned toward Adele.

"Not Adele! She only came here when he was already sick and not likely to cause mischief. But I hired her specifically because of her impeccable resume and talents and because she so resembles me that I knew she'd be the last person he would lay eyes on." She laughed at this, and Adele looked down at her plate to disguise the flush of her cheeks.

"Mother...," Caroline scolded.

"Don't *Mother* me. What if I were to tell you that I'm not your mother?"

"I would say you are being horrible as usual."

"Well, I may be horrible but what I say is true. Dear Daddy seduced Vera, two assistants before you, Adele, who became pregnant, and she and I went away on a long holiday. She helped me finish my book, I paid for the maternity expenses while we were in Maine, and she gave me the lovely Caroline."

"You are making this up," Caroline said without emotion.

"Mother did go away for a long vacation before you were born and came back with a baby girl. Maybe it is true," Allan said.

"Were you so dense that you didn't put it together or ask questions? You were seven or eight at the time. Were you always so thick? Besides, I think she is lying just to irk me, and you are lying because you hope that I will no longer count as an heir to the Browne fortune."

Hextilda laughed. "The Browne fortune. Who knows how much of it is left? My advice, dear children, is to sell off this pile and all the stuff in it, take the money and run."

"You do have an accountant, don't you?" Allan asked, looking horrified.

"Oh, yes, that lawyer fellow. I suppose once we have telephone service again I ought to call him."

"And include us in the discussion, if you don't mind," he added. "We have a right to know what is going on."

"You've badgered me enough for the day about what to do. I'll meet with him and ask his advice about including any of you."

Fred played with the silverware at his place setting. "Mother, perhaps it's time for bed."

"I take the challenge, Mother. Let me see my birth certificate."

"I don't know where it is...."

"Now I think you are bluffing. Isn't this a charming family you are thinking of marrying into, José?" Caroline said.

"Marrying? I thought he was just your most recent plaything until the next handsome charmer came your way." Hextilda pushed herself up from the table. "The good advice this evening from Dr. Frederick is to go to bed. And so I shall." She teetered out of the room, reaching out to balance herself at the doorway.

Caroline began to cry. "Why must she be so hateful? Is it because she had a horrible marriage and she had to work so hard to get where she is? Or is it because I look like Vera?" She directed this last question at Allan who reacted with surprise.

"I don't remember what she looked like except that she was pretty and very nice to me. She may have had blonde hair like you, I really can't remember."

"Worthless," she said, throwing her napkin onto the table. "That's what Daddy called you and he was right." She grabbed a candle out of the candelabra and left the room, José scrambling to catch up.

Allan glared at us across the table. "My father never called me worthless." He pushed his chair back from the table and stormed out.

We were either looking at each other or down at our plates. Fred swirled the wine in his glass and took a drink. "I don't think I need to say how embarrassed I am by my family's behavior. I can assure you it is not usually like this, and it won't be like this again. Merry Ersatz Christmas, everyone!"

Chapter Nineteen

"What in the world was Fred talking about—Ersatz Christmas?" Julia asked me as we got ready for bed.

"It's almost too ridiculous to explain. Hextilda had the idea to gather her children together and John and me for some reason, for a family holiday celebration. It seems to have been little more than a way to ferret out their feelings about her."

"I wonder why?"

I shrugged. "She is getting older, seems to have waning enthusiasm in her writing or perhaps the public has less interest in her work, perhaps both."

"Gosh, that's sad."

I had put my pajamas on and, grabbing my robe, asked her if the ankle still hurt.

"Just a little bit. But I don't want to take any pain medication for it."

"Maybe a nightcap would be just the thing. Let me rustle up some whiskey. That shouldn't be hard in this household."

The fire was tamped down, but I could find the decanter well enough with my trusty flashlight. I filled two glasses partway up, took them in one hand and the light in the other and made my way back upstairs and through the partially open bedroom door.

"No ice, of course, although we could just reach out the window for snow. Let me get some water from the washroom," I said, putting the glasses on the nightstand between the beds.

I smiled at the recollection of nurses' training where despite Prohibition one of us invariably found an alcohol source for an impromptu Saturday night get-together in someone's room, a gleeful but quiet event so Head Nurse Watson wouldn't hear us. Those were fun times with Glenda the life of the party doing impersonations of the various teachers and doctors. She must find the life of a housewife to be a great deal more boring unless she kept up with some of the gals or had as exciting a social life as her husband intimated.

When I got back, I carefully poured a bit of water into Julia's glass and mine, we clinked and took a sip.

I grimaced. "I shouldn't have brushed my teeth first," I said. "Pepsodent and whiskey do not taste good together."

"Maybe you have invented a new drink: the Brighter Whiskey."

I took a sip of the water before taking another drink of the alcohol. "That's better."

"I'm sorry if I sounded harsh about the family. The Brownes have been very generous in putting us up," Julia said.

"Whatever you may think, they weren't about to leave you out in the storm to fend for yourselves."

"Still, I can't wait to get out of here. The place is kind of creepy. I can see why they might want to sell it. On a personal level, I am getting a bit tired of wearing this assortment of hand-me-down clothes. If that doesn't sound too ungracious of me." She peered over the top of the glass but didn't look very contrite.

I laughed. "I understand entirely. As they say, tomorrow is another day, and we may be able to leave. If John and Fred could walk out to the main road, so can I. Don't worry, I'll send for reinforcements."

Julia picked up a magazine and leafed through it by candlelight while I tried to concentrate on Alistair's latest difficulties. The poor man had been shot at, pummeled, fallen off a cliff—what else could he endure? I wasn't to find out that Sunday night.

* * *

I awoke to the blazing light of the sun on the snow outside the window and all the lights on in the room. It took me a moment to realize that I had fallen asleep thinking about Scotland, slept soundly through the night, that it was a full morning and the electricity was back on.

"Fantastic!" I said, perhaps too loudly as Julia stirred and asked what had happened.

"We can ditch the flashlights. We have power."

She sat up and looked around. "It is awfully bright. Do you think the snow might be melting, too?"

I got up and looked out the window. "It's kind of hard to say. I can see that Bruce has done more shoveling, that's a good thing. It would be wonderful if the telephone were working."

"Oh, yes, will you go and see?"

I put on my robe and slippers and went down to the library where I had seen a telephone and picking up the receiver heard a click.

"Operator. Is this you, Adele?"

"I'm sorry, it's not. I'm a guest at the house and I was wondering if the phones were working."

"Yes, they are, and everybody is anxious to use them."

"I beg your pardon," I said and hung up feeling guilty for having wasted her time but relieved that we might be able to get some assistance with Joan's murder as well as get ourselves out of there. I also wanted to call Miss Manley and let her know all was well and perhaps have her put a note on the doctor's door that he wouldn't be in that day. What a silly notion—of course, he wouldn't be in, and it was just as likely that West Adams was snowed in and without telephone service.

I went back upstairs, washed up, got dressed and asked Julia if she needed any assistance but she refused, and I saw that she moved easily and was even putting some weight on the injured foot.

"Good for you, I'm going to let John know about the lights and the phones. Probably everybody in the region has had difficulties with power and it's going to take some time to dig out."

John was exiting his room with a big smile on his face just as I got there. "Let there be light!" he exclaimed and gave me a resounding kiss on the cheek.

"And the phones are working, too."

He rubbed his hands together in anticipation of a day of action. "Time to get the car in working order. We may not be able to drive out safely just yet and the main road was well covered with snow, but we may as well try."

"I was just telling Julia that if you and Fred got out to the main road, you and I could walk out, too." I laughed but I was a bit serious.

"It would be wonderful to leave this all behind, but we probably shouldn't leave until the sheriff gets here."

"Yes, I know. If we can't get out, how will he be able to get in?"

He shrugged. "I smell coffee and am starving."

Fred was already in the dining room, also all smiles at the turn of events. "It's only been two days, but it seems like we've been here for a week. I don't want to see another flashlight for a long time."

"I wonder if this storm hit Boston, too, in which case it will be hard for you to get back. Were you expected to be on duty today?"

"No, I had taken several more days of leave than that. I anticipated leaving today or tomorrow and having another few days to myself back home. Oh, well."

We heard a distant ring of the telephone, which abruptly stopped.

"Oh, dear, I hope it hasn't stopped working," I said.

I took a good portion of eggs and sausage and, while deciding on whether I needed to have bacon as well, Eleanor came into the dining room.

"That was the sheriff. He said he got your message and would be coming down soon. More coffee?"

I picked up the silver pot and let her know there was plenty there.

Allan came in shortly thereafter with bags under his eyes, followed by Kent and Julia, who still had the crutches to steady her walk. They had barely had time to sit down before a scream pierced the air and the brothers ran down the hall toward Hextilda's wing with everyone but Julia following.

Allan threw open the door of the study to see a female figure slumped over the desk with the sgian-dubh sticking out of her back.

"Mother!" Allan shouted.

"I'm here," she answered from behind the door.

He looked at her in astonishment and back to the body at the desk, then gingerly put his hand on the shoulder of the body and withdrew it quickly.

"It's Adele. And she's dead."

"I told you there was a curse on the family, but you wouldn't listen!" Hextilda accused her son.

"What has Adele got to do with the family curse?" Fred asked.

We stared for a few moments.

"She's wearing the same clothes she had on last night," I observed.

"Then she never went to bed," Allan commented needlessly.

"How could she have been stabbed? That damned dagger was hidden in my room," John said.

"Not well enough, unless there is more than one."

"No, only the one," Hextilda confirmed.

Silence again.

We heard footsteps behind us as Eleanor and Bruce crowded into the doorway.

"The poor girl," she muttered.

142

"The sheriff will be here sometime this morning. Let's leave things as they are. Mother, come have some coffee or something to eat. You look dreadful," Allan said.

He helped her back to the dining room where Julia sat, wide-eyed, waiting to hear what had happened. Seeing the solemn procession come in, her hand flew to her mouth.

"It's Adele. She's dead."

"What?"

"I'd better not say anymore. Mother is terribly upset. Here, sit down." He eased her into the chair at the head of the table and scowled at the rest of us. "I don't know what all this means." He turned to the sideboard to pour coffee for his mother, but she put her hand on his arm.

"Whiskey," was all she said.

Allan hurried into the Great Room and came back quickly with the decanter and poured a sizeable amount into an empty coffee cup.

John took the cup from her hand. "Can somebody get a sweater or a blanket?"

Since everyone seemed dazed, I guessed I was the somebody and rushed back into the Great Room, took the woolen afghan off the sofa and quickly returned to put it around her shoulders.

"You're pale and stunned. Let's make sure you are comfortable. Then perhaps some coffee would be all right."

One by one we sat down, looking at the cold remains of the breakfast on the table although the burner under the chafing dish was still lit. I hated to admit it, much less say it, but I was still hungry.

"Let me see if we can get some hot coffee for everyone." I went down the hall to the kitchen and saw Eleanor and Bruce sitting side by side at the table in the middle of the room, looking stricken. I had not realized that they had been so fond of Adele, but she had told me she'd been here four years, enough time to be comfortable with each other.

"I hate to interrupt, but could you get some tea and coffee for everyone? I think it might help."

She showed no emotion as she moved toward the stove to get the kettle and fill it with water. I slipped out quietly to join the others.

It was one of those times where you feel any appearance of normalcy will somehow make things normal and sometimes those attempts seem awkward and forced but I plowed on.

"Can I get you something to eat?" I asked Hextilda.

She shook her head.

I sat back down and picked up a piece of cold toast from my plate and nibbled at it as if eating any more heartily would be offensive.

"Why Adele?" Hextilda asked. Her color was returning as was her temper. "It's almost as if you all have been trying to take away my means of writing entirely. Comments about the waning interest in my books, snide remarks about my characters, references to bodice-ripping, it has been endless. Stop writing! Sell the house! Go into a corner and dry up in a ball and blow away!"

Nobody responded and the minutes ticked away as I stared longingly at the untouched sausage on my plate. At last, the coffee and tea came, which to my mind gave permission to resume eating. The quirk in John's eyebrow told me that he couldn't understand how I had an appetite at a time like this.

Fred stood. "I think I'll help Bruce with the shoveling."

"Good idea," John agreed and got up. "Just going to put on some sturdy clothes," he added.

Kent looked around the room and shrugged. "Guess I'll help."

José said nothing but he and Allen, left, too.

"Would you like to lie down?" I asked Hextilda.

"Perhaps in the library," she answered. I think she was hesitant to go to her room, which would have meant passing her study and the sorrowful sight of Adele.

Caroline took her mother away and just Julia and I were left in the dining room.

"Sorry, I'm hungry," I apologized, digging into my food with renewed gusto.

"What a horrible place this is." She got up using one crutch as a cane and left me to myself.

After eating more than I should have, I weighed my options of what to do next. My curiosity got the best of me and, looking up and down the hallway for any signs of activity, I walked softly toward Hextilda's study, wanting to examine the dagger more closely. How could someone have ransacked John's room and found it? One answer was that he may have hidden it in an obvious place. But another answer was that Allan was still sharing a room with him and he either saw it hidden away or had plenty of time to look through the room while John was doing something else.

The door to the study was partially closed and I opened it carefully hoping that nobody else was in the room. Poor Adele. Her murder made no sense at all unless she was privy to some information or knowledge that someone didn't want her to have. I walked carefully to the side of the desk, keeping about a foot away in the event there were some clues that the sheriff might need to find. I could see Adele was bent over some papers and I squinted to see if I could read them. A will? A confession?

No, it seemed to be typewritten pages that had editing marks on them. The next book in the series that Hextilda was anxious to get finished. It looked like Adele sat down after dinner to resume work on it, something she probably did with regularity. Something someone in this house was familiar with and took advantage of. I walked back and took a closer look at the dagger without touching it. It looked just like the one that Hextilda brandished when talking of the Comyn curse and all that other nonsense.

Only it wasn't nonsense any longer.

I heard an ominous banging noise from the direction of the Great Room and once my heart stopped beating so fast, I realized someone had come to the front door. I left the study, went through the hallway and could see Eleanor retreating to the library while before me stood a strapping young man, red flannel hat in hand, his blonde hair flopping into his face even as he looked up at the imposing furnishings and enormity of the Great Hall.

"Are you the sheriff?" I asked.

He smiled and came forward holding out his hand. "Not really. I guess you could say I'm one of the deputies."

I shook his hand. "*Are* you one of the deputies?"

"I'm Ray Robinson. My father, Big Ray, is the sheriff. He's got a touch of the flu, so he asked me to come out instead."

I knew we were in rural Vermont, but it still seemed overly casual for the head law enforcement officer to send his son in his place. I couldn't think of anything to say.

"I'm awful sorry to hear about what happened, Miss Browne." He twisted his hat in his hands to indicate his sincerity.

"I'm Miss Browne," Caroline said rather haughtily as she approached from the archway that led toward the library.

He stammered a bit more, looking first to her and then to me and finally said, "I guess I'm supposed to look at the body. Of the deceased," he clarified.

By this time the men had come into the room and Ray's head spun from one to the other trying to figure out who was who and I was surprised that he hadn't met any of them before realizing that they only visited occasionally.

"Which one?" Allan asked.

"My father, Big Ray, got a message delivered yesterday after the storm about a death in the house that might be suspicious."

Caroline scoffed. "If you consider a dagger in the chest suspicious, yes." She sat down.

"That would qualify," he said seriously.

"It was my wife, Joan," Allan said. "Come, I'll show you."

He led the young man out of the Great Room and into the hallway that led to the cellar.

Caroline shivered. "Do you think he is even sixteen? Isn't there someone more senior who can be called in?"

I immediately thought of Inspector Gladstone, but he was in Pittsfield, Massachusetts, and it would be out of his jurisdiction.

"The County Sheriff is an elected position," Fred explained. "He gets a vehicle, a badge and a portion of any tickets he can issue to tourists for speeding along Route 7 or 8 after the County Clerk, also elected, collects the administrative fees. The Robinsons have had a lock on the sheriff position for several generations."

John and I looked at one another in surprise. And we thought West Adams and Adams were the epitome of small-town America.

"I think that means there is not only a Big Ray but there might have been a Big Big Ray at some point," John said.

"Old Man Robinson, if you please," Fred explained.

We sat and waited for the local lawman to return, which he did more quickly than I would have imagined.

"That's terrible. And I'm sorry for your loss. Can you tell me where the weapon is?"

John rubbed his nose with his hand in embarrassment, but Fred answered.

"It was in safekeeping but evidently stolen. And used again."

"What?"

We could hear their footsteps as Fred led him to his mother's study and then stopped shortly inside the door. We looked at one another, Caroline shaking her head. Allan paced the floor.

"We can't just leave her body in there," she said.

"What do you recommend we do?"

Her silence gave him the answer.

"Let her keep Joan company, you mean?" Allan asked ferociously.

"Just until the funeral home can take them," she said in a quiet voice.

He exhaled loudly and twisted his head as if to release the tension.

"If Ray could get in, so can someone else," she reasoned. "And these people can go home."

"What? As much as we'd like to, nobody has been formally questioned and I hardly think that young man is capable of such a thing," I said.

"We'll have to stay until this is concluded," John said.

My shoulders sank in frustration even though I knew it was necessary.

Fred came back in, and Young Ray announced, "I've just called my father and let him know that he's needed."

Big Ray was on the way.

Chapter Twenty

I had no concept of what Bennington County looked like except what I had seen out the window of John's car and that was of a mostly rural area with lots of cows, but surely there must be a larger town than Stamford. I was informed by Fred that Bennington itself was the largest town and, although the county was a 'good size' as he put it, the sheriff lived outside of that city not too far away and should be with us within the hour. I wasn't looking forward to spending another day in that house, but it was unavoidable, and I did not want to be in the company of someone with the flu.

Big Ray was just that, a larger, older version of his son and it seemed he only had a head cold and was not keen on being called out on short notice.

"Where's Mrs. Browne?" he asked. "I've met her before. Isn't she here?"

"I'll get her," Caroline said, fetching her mother from the library.

Hextilda and the sheriff shook hands, and he expressed his condolences.

"May I sit down?"

"Certainly."

He reached into the pocket of his jacket and pulled out an envelope to write on with a stubby pencil, then began by asking who was in the house when Joan died—he didn't use the term murdered and she reeled off the names of her children, José, who had just come in from outside, John and me, Kent and Julia, at which he raised his bushy eyebrows, when it was explained how they came to be there, the Mowbrays, and Mariah and Nancy. We waited while he laboriously wrote down the names, asking for clarification on the spelling of some.

He exhaled, took out a handkerchief and blew his nose and asked to see the body, presumably Joan's. Allan had the sad job of escorting Big Ray to the basement, his son in tow, and they returned a few minutes later. By the looks the two Rays gave each other, it seemed as if they had no clue how to proceed.

"We'd better see the other deceased," Big Ray said. Off they went to Hextilda's study, and we sat or stood in the Great Room wondering what was expected of us next. Naturally, I thought they would retrieve the dagger and take it somewhere to look for fingerprints, but this rural area probably didn't have something as sophisticated as a laboratory for such things. If they needed to get something like that done, they would have to hand-deliver it to—Burlington, perhaps? All kinds of contamination of evidence could take place during the transfer and the prints of whoever killed Joan, if they were so stupid as not to use gloves, were obliterated or blurred by the second killer. If there were two.

Someone had been very clever in carrying out the nasty deeds here during a raging snowstorm and where detecting techniques were not sophisticated. And judging by the interest or competence of the Robinsons, the murders might never be solved. The men came back into the room looking utterly defeated by two murders in one house with one weapon, no clues and a houseful of suspects.

"I guess we should begin by asking where everyone was the night that the late Mrs. Browne died," Big Ray said.

"We were all in our respective bedrooms," Caroline answered.

"Except for Allan, who had a disagreement with Joan and spent the night in the spare bed with Doctor Taylor."

John raised his hand at this point to indicate who she was referring to. "Yes, he asked to spend the night and to my knowledge that is exactly what he did."

"Who found the body?"

"I did," Eleanor said from the doorway.

"Everyone wondered why she hadn't come down to breakfast and I went up to see. The door was locked, and I found a key."

"Who else had a key to that room?"

"There was one inside somewhere, but we are not in the habit of locking the door," Allan said.

"Did your wife fear violence against her after your disagreement?" Big Ray asked.

"Certainly not!" Allan protested.

"If it's of any use, they *disagreed* often," Caroline said. Her brother shot her a venomous look, but she held her hands out as if to indicate that everyone was aware of the fact.

"Doctor Taylor, can you describe the scene in the bedroom?"

"The thing that struck me was that the windows were wide open, and the radiator was turned off, making the room icy cold. There was no way Fred—also a physician—or I could have estimated time of death accurately."

"So, we can say she died sometime during the night."

We all looked at each other and I wondered if he were looking for some group consensus but said nothing.

"It would appear so," Fred said.

Big Ray chewed his lower lip as he thought, and he wrote again on the envelope.

"Now, the young woman who was found in the room back there...."

"My study," Hextilda clarified.

"When was she last seen?"

"Sometime after dinner last night. She took her work very seriously and was working on the latest draft of my book, checking through additions and strikethroughs. I had gone to bed already and I had no idea she was still working."

Big Ray looked around at each of us and settled his gaze on Kent and Julia. "I don't understand. What are you two doing here?"

Their faces flushed in the same manner, and they looked at each other. "We were hiking, and the storm started. We got lost on our way back to our car and Mr. Mowbray found us and brought us here."

"Do you own a Ford?"

"Yes, I do," Kent said, relieved. "I didn't imagine anyone would steal it, but we lost our way back to the main road and couldn't find it."

"You're lucky the snowplow didn't hit it," Young Ray said.

"What were you doing hiking out here?"

Kent stammered. "Looking at the scenery, birds, you know. Just exercise."

The bushy eyebrows went up. If you were a farmer or worked with your hands, the last thing you had time for was a walk in the woods. In December. In a place you had never been before.

"Where was everyone last night after dinner?"

"As far as I know, everyone went to their rooms," Allan said.

"I have to admit that I came back downstairs to get a nightcap for Julia and me. She said that her ankle was bothering her, and I thought it was a simple sedative."

John looked at me questioningly and I shrugged as if to let him know that no harm was done.

Kent's face flushed again. "I hate to say this, but José and I did not share a room last night, at least not all night."

José's eyes flashed at the young man. "What do you mean?"

Kent stammered and Caroline broke in. "If you must know, José spent part of the night with me. That means that Kent was by himself or unaccounted for, I would say." She tossed her head in triumph.

"I just met that woman the other day! What are you suggesting?"

"I leave it to the authorities to come to conclusions," José said loftily.

Bruce, who had been out of the room most of the time, came back in to say that the funeral home van from Bennington had come and it brought us back to sober, practical thoughts.

Big Ray got up. "Well, don't anybody go anywhere just yet. At the moment it seems like a person or persons unknown were responsible for the deaths of the two women." He nodded to Hextilda, whose mouth was open in surprise.

"That's it?" she asked.

"That's it for now until we know more," Big Ray said.

John and I went to the Game Room, certain that no one would follow us there.

"That's it?" I asked him.

"He has no idea what he is doing. Maybe he doesn't want to anger one of the largest—if not the richest—landowners in the area."

We sat down on the sofa across from the billiard table. "Let's start at the beginning. Why are we all here?" I asked.

"Because Hextilda Browne said she felt threatened and wanted as many people as possible here."

"To witness something? To prevent something? Or to provide cover for something she planned to do?"

"The first night seemed like she wanted to uncover the motivations of her children. The second night...."

"That was when she got the threatening message in the cookie. Do you think she could have planted that herself? But why? To throw suspicion on someone else?" I asked.

"But why kill Joan? It seemed she was not fond of her, but why kill her? How would that benefit Hextilda?"

"Not at all. Do you think it was done that night after a fight to throw suspicion on Allan?"

"He would be the most likely suspect. But if Caroline...."

"Or Fred...," I added.

"Wanted to knock someone out of the line of inheritance, that would be a way to do it."

We were quiet for a few moments.

"But why kill Adele? It makes no sense."

"I agree," John said. "By the way, why did Julia have a nightcap instead of using the Tincture of Opium I left for her.

"She never told me she had it."

"Let's see if it's in your room."

We went upstairs and not caring how it looked, I turned the lock on the bedroom door behind us to give us privacy to search for the opium. The chest of drawers held only those few clothes that Caroline had lent her, and the night table had a magazine in the drawer and our two nightcap glasses on top.

John sniffed in the glasses. "Phew, here's your opium tincture," he said.

"Wait, that was my glass, not hers. Maybe that's why I went to sleep so quickly and deeply all night. Do you think she meant it for herself and got the glasses mixed up?"

"You mean you think she is a drug addict?" John asked. "She doesn't fit the description at all. But women have been overusing the opiate laudanum for years."

I got down on my hands and knees, pulled up the dust ruffle on the bed and looked underneath. "Hand me the flashlight," I asked, and once turned on, far in the corner where the leg of the bed met the floor was the tiny bottle. I wiggled underneath the bed and produced it.

"Look, it's nearly full."

John took it from me, sniffed at it and said, "It may look full, but I believe she may have diluted it with water so I wouldn't know any was gone until we got back to West Adams and I needed to use it again."

The doorknob rattled and I got up to unlock the door.

"Sorry," I said. Julia looked at me curiously.

John held up the bottle saying nothing.

"I was looking for that! Where did you find it?"

"Under the bed where you put it," I said.

She looked from one of us to the other and began to stammer, then got her senses back and came up with a plausible explanation. "I took the medicine as you suggested for pain and, well, it felt so good, I'm afraid I took it when I didn't entirely need it."

"People sometimes do that," he said calmly.

"But why did you put it into my glass of whiskey last night?"

"I certainly did not," she said.

"It smells like there was some in this glass," John continued.

"I don't smell anything," she said. She was not going to admit it.

"Very well. Since José was in Caroline's bedroom last night and probably every night, I would suggest that you sleep in the room with your brother. I don't feel safe with you here."

"Fine," she said, greatly offended. She limped over to the chest to retrieve the clothes and stumbled dramatically.

"Here, are you all right?" John asked.

She began to cry, and I tried with all my might not to roll my eyes in disbelief. I didn't know what her game was, but I wasn't falling for it.

"I'll help you take those down the hall," I said, scooping up the sweaters and socks while she made a show of humping slowly behind me on the crutches.

I ungraciously dumped the clothes on one of the beds and saw a packet of cigarettes on the night table. I hadn't seen Kent or José smoking. They were Lucky Strikes. I left her to sort things out on her own and slammed the door behind me.

I had seen a crumpled packet in the boathouse the other day. Even if Hextilda didn't approve of the habit, there was no one in the house who smoked except Caroline, and she didn't hesitate to do so in front of her mother.

Then the thought occurred to me that maybe they were Kent's cigarettes, and it was he who had been in the boathouse. That's where Kent and Julia were before they came out to the main road to be rescued by Bruce. Were they casing the house intending to steal something? Kent's story of being a teacher seemed implausible, but what were they up to? And how did they even know the location of Browne's Castle?

I went back to my room where John sat on one of the beds.

"Alone at last," he said.

"John, this is not the time. I want to talk to you."

He was all ears. "I think Kent and Julia have had something to do with all this. I found this in his room, and I don't think they are José's. Remember we saw some down at the boathouse? Along with some cans of food and blankets. What if Kent had been hiding out there or at least visiting, trying to determine the best time to carry out his scheme?"

"What scheme was that?"

"I don't know."

I sat down next to him. "Who gains by Joan's death? No one. Who gains by Adele's death? No one."

"Despite his sad looks, I think Allan is certainly better off without arguing with his wife all the time."

"Someone made mention of her family's money," I suggested.

"Perhaps there was a life insurance policy," John suggested.

My eyes opened wide. "Guess who works at an insurance company? Julia. She told me at breakfast."

"That doesn't explain why Adele was killed."

"Wait a minute. Adele and Hextilda often switched sitting at one desk or another. What if Adele was not the intended victim but Hextilda? It was dark, there was only the light of a candle because the electricity was still not working, the two women had the same kind of hairstyle..."

"Allan would surely recognize his own mother," John said.

"What if it wasn't Allan who killed Adele? What if it was Julia?"

"With her ankle in bad shape?"

"It may have been initially, but it seemed to have healed quickly enough for her to get around. It's only when someone is paying attention that she takes the crutches out for show. What if she and Allan are in this together? Allan gets the life insurance money and his mother out of the way all in the space of a weekend. If Allan 'happens' to fall in love with Julia, they can pretend it was as a consequence of this dreadful weekend here, not that they have been carrying on all along."

"That is some theory!" John said.

"Yes, but how can we prove it?"

"We can't. Unless someone is going to make an attempt on Hextilda's life. We need to warn her."

"I think we need to set a trap," I said.

"Oh, no, Aggie. I hope you don't have the idea of luring whoever it is into putting her in jeopardy."

"Of course not! I have the brilliant idea of pretending to be Hextilda and making him or her or them think it will be easy to get away with another murder. Here's my plan," I said.

Chapter Twenty-One

Of course, John tried to dissuade me, and although I ought to have been wary of trying to outsmart someone very clever and calculating, I had begun to take this business seriously, even if Big Ray didn't seem to. I tracked down Young Ray, who was moseying around the garage, admiring an antique automobile covered by canvas back in the shadows and deep in conversation with Bruce, who was describing all of the car's attributes in great detail. John had already asked for a jump to get his battery charged again and I saw that the cables were in Bruce's hands, ready for the task. Too bad we hadn't been able to utilize them earlier.

I pulled Young Ray aside and let him know that Hextilda wished him to spend the night but not to tell the others that he was doing so.

"Not to be so blunt, but if you could eat dinner in the kitchen just to keep out of sight."

"Sure thing, Miss," he said, probably glad to have an excellent meal and not have to deal with that strange family.

We walked back along the path through the snow toward the mudroom entrance.

"Being a small community, I guess everyone here knows everyone else," I said.

"Oh, sure. Mr. Mowbray and my dad go way back. They used to hunt with Mr. Browne."

"So those antlers—racks—were from local hunting trips?"

"Oh, yeah," he said. "Mr. Browne was out and about every chance he could get. The last time he did, he was by himself. That's why nobody ever found out who shot him."

I stopped dead in my tracks.

"I thought he had died of some illness?"

"Nope. He had been sick for some time but wouldn't miss going out hunting."

We had reached the back door and carefully stomped what snow there was off our boots. He kept his on and took a seat in the kitchen and I removed mine to let them dry and made my way to the library where John was bent over a game of chess with Fred. I would just have to tell John what I learned later though I was bursting to tell him right then.

I found Hextilda in her study although not at either of the desks, but at a window seat, shuffling through the piles of a manuscript. She seemed dazed by Adele's death, more so than that of her daughter-in-law, so I decided to stay with her for a while.

"You know, I think that all this business is about trying to stop me from writing. To throw me off my stride, sideline me, then get me out of the way."

I didn't see what that had to do with Joan's death although the correlation with Adele's held water.

"We'll get to the bottom of this tonight, I think," I said, and I told her what I had in mind and saw the spark come back into her eyes.

"Aren't you clever?" Then thinking a bit, she added, "Due to the circumstances, I'll let everyone know we're having an informal, buffet-style meal tonight. It will take a bit of burden off Eleanor and the others and there will be no folderol about Ersatz Christmas." She gave a bit of a smile at that point and got up to do just that. "And we're all so tired that we'll go to bed early. How's that?"

I nodded. I certainly hoped this would work.

Dinner was a quiet meal and Hextilda excused herself early saying she was not feeling well. After dinner, we had the usual whiskey drinks and I made sure to shoot daggers with my eyes at Julia after the discovery of what was in my nightcap last night, but she was brazen enough to pretend not to notice my sharp looks. The conversation was minimal, mostly about when Big Ray might return tomorrow and when we might be able to get back to our normal lives, a discussion I found unfeeling under the circumstances.

"I hope your office doesn't have a problem with your being gone so long," I said to Julia.

"I'm sure they will understand," she said.

"Aren't you lucky to have such an understanding boss," I replied.

She gave a small smile and went to great lengths to thank Caroline for the clothing and the hospitality, John and Fred for their medical attention and then blatantly me, for being the best roommate ever.

One by one, we said our goodnights and made our way upstairs and I made a great fuss of getting my washbag and taking my time in the big bathroom to make sure everyone else was tucked in for the night. Looking over the gallery railing, I could see that Julia, Kent, Fred and Allan were still in the Great Room chatting and I would have to wait for them to go to bed, so it was just me and Alistair.

A tap on the door and John eased himself through the opening.

"Did anyone see you?" I asked. "Is everyone still downstairs?"

"No. I heard the doors open and close. I've got a pillow person under covers in my bed although Allan had moved his stuff back into his bedroom earlier today."

"Perfect."

"Come on, you need a pillow person, too," he said, and we positioned two end-to-end and covered what should be me with blankets, rumpling them to look more authentic in the event someone came to check on me.

"Let's go."

We crept down the hallway, alert to any noises or eyes upon us, down the stairway, through the hall to Hextilda's wing and up the stairs to her room. I tapped on the door and heard nothing. I tapped again. Silence.

I quietly opened the door to an enormous bedroom with a full-sized bed up against the wall and a body lying still.

"Oh, no!" I said.

"Damn!" John whispered.

We both rushed over and put our hands out to find that it was not Hextilda's body, but another pillow person.

"Where is she?"

"I couldn't find her," Young Ray said from behind the door.

I almost jumped out of my skin.

"I made it look like she was there instead."

"That wasn't the plan," I said.

"I'm here," Hextilda whispered, opening the closet.

"That wasn't the plan, either," I said.

"I'm sorry, what should we do now?" she asked.

"I need your hairnet, and I need you to get back in the closet with John. Don't move and don't make a sound."

"I don't like this," Young Ray said.

"Neither do I," I admitted, going to her vanity, putting some cream on my face and a net over my bobbed hair. I slipped her night-gown over my clothes and got into the bed with the covers up close to my chin. John, Ray and Hextilda went into the closet.

The long wait began.

I was too keyed up to fall asleep, but I was afraid I might none-theless, so I decided to remember the mnemonics for the cranial nerves, one that was such a trial for me in nurses' training: On Old Olympus's Towering Top, A Finn And German Viewed Some Hops. Olfactory nerve, optic nerve, oculomotor, trochlear, trigeminal, abducent, facial, auditory, glossopharyngeal, vagus, spinal accessory, hypoglossal. *Not bad, Aggie,* I thought. It had been less than a year since our finals, but I thought for sure that information would have seeped out of my brain already. The day-to-day work of nursing never involved using those terms, much less identifying them.

Now what? I listened carefully in the dim room where there was only a small night light on the other side and moved my legs a bit.

What should it be now, Presidents of the United States, state capitals, not my strong point, French irregular verbs? I remembered some little song that our fifth-grade teacher taught us to be able to recite the presidents and I was almost to Fillmore when I got the sensation that someone was in the room, although not a sound had been made. True, the room was carpeted, but I had expected to hear a door creak or some noise, not the abrupt smashing of a pillow on my face.

I screamed but was sure that it was entirely muffled, I flailed my arms, punching at what should be a face and only hit strong arms that continued the pressure.

Couldn't John hear me? Where was Ray?

I finally did the one thing my mother taught me to do as a teenager in the event of 'you know what,' and I brought both knees up sharply, hitting someone squarely in the groin as a shuffle and tussle indicated that my assailant had fallen on the ground and been tackled.

I turned the light on.

John and Ray held Allan Browne down on the ground by the shoulders while his mother looked down at him with sorrow, horror and disappointment.

"Now what?" John asked.

Young Ray said, "My father has been out in the garage waiting. If you can hold onto Mr. Browne here, I'll go get him. He's got the firepower." He left the room at a trot.

I took my time taking off the nightgown and the hairnet and

coughed a bit, which caught John's attention for the split second that Allan pushed him out of the way and ran toward the door.

"No!" I yelled, racing after him, John getting up and following close behind. We had reached the head of the stairs and I slipped in my stocking feet on the wood and hurtled head-first down the stairs, smashing into Allan, the both of us landing in a heap on the landing.

John came thundering down the stairs as the Rays stormed up and kept Allan at bay while I checked for injuries. Torn stockings, probably a broken pinky finger, bumped head, but otherwise, fairly intact.

Allan had taken the impact of my body and by his moans had suffered more. Without an ounce of remorse, I felt no pity whatsoever.

We took him to the Great Room, by which time the entire household was up and assembling and Big Ray sat to begin his relentless inquiry.

"I guess we got you red-handed," Big Ray said.

The others looked at Allan, not yet understanding what happened.

"He thought I was Hextilda and he tried to smother me."

Gasps around the room.

"Allan, say it isn't true," Caroline said.

"I'm not saying anything."

"Well, I'll say it. It is true and Doctor Taylor, Young Ray and your mother all witnessed it."

Silence.

"Furthermore, I believe that Allan killed his wife. He created that argument and made a show of leaving their bedroom and staying in the room with John. After spiking John's drink with the opium Julia had been given, he waited until his roommate was unconscious, went back and killed Joan with the dagger just to excite everyone's attention about the so-called curse."

"How did he get hold of Julia's pain medication?" José asked.

"She gave it to him willingly. My guess is that their relationship began after he met her at the insurance company where she works when he tried to cash out Joan's insurance policy because money was so tight. Then the thought occurred to him that it would be better all-around if Joan were dead so he could collect the entire amount."

"But why did he kill Adele?" Hextilda asked.

"He didn't," I said. "Julia was tasked with killing Hextilda so no one would suspect Allan. They wanted to fully realize their dreams of being financially independent. Sell the house here, sell the Boston house."

"I would never sell the Boston house," Allan protested.

"The problem was not that Julia had a twisted ankle, no, that seemed to be healing very well unless she wanted to appear helpless. The real problem was that despite Kent's having hidden out in the boathouse for some time to see the rhythm of the household and get a layout of the rooms, he was unaware of the working habits of Hextilda and Adele, who would often switch places at the facing desks while working. Julia spiked my nightcap with the opium, too, so I was out cold all night. She got up, used the dagger that Allan had taken from wherever in the room John had hidden it and went to the study to kill Hextilda. All she could see in the candlelight was a woman seated at the desk facing away from her and her assumption was it was Allan's mother. She struck quickly and went back to bed. It was only the next morning when Hextilda was escorted back into the dining room that she realized her mistake. Allan had to finish the job and tonight was the night. She would have been found in her bed, likely dead of a heart attack after all the sorrow of the past few days."

"That's ridiculous," Julia said.

"We can prove that Kent had been in the boathouse and was probably the figure that some of us saw in the woods. The notion that you two were hiking was absurd."

"Furthermore, and this might seem like a small matter, but I don't believe for an instant that you are a teacher anywhere," Fred said.

"Thank you," Big Ray said. "I think we have a strong case against Allan and perhaps our little songbird would like to sing to save herself." He looked over at Julia, who held her head high in defiance. She might be a tough nut to crack but Kent was positively squirming under the gaze of the furious family and the relentless Big Ray.

"Perhaps Kent would like to share some information?" Big Ray asked sweetly.

"Kent has the least to lose of the three of them, having only trespassed and lied. Unless you considered an accessory after the fact," John added.

"Don't you dare say a word!" Julia screamed at her brother.

He was quiet but it seemed to me that once by himself and weighing the odds, he would be the one to sing.

Chapter Twenty-Two

Big Ray brought the three conspirators to Burlington, the closest place that could jail all three of them before trial. We stayed one more day at Browne's Castle, the sorrowful atmosphere permeating everything so that what should have been relief at the snowmelt that allowed us to safely leave felt like we were abandoning our hostess.

Caroline admitted that her gallery was already a financial loss and agreed to take her mother back to Boston and stay with her there until she could settle things in New York. Hextilda wandered about the house the last day we were there as if trying to remember why she had held on to the house as long as she had. It seemed she might sell Browne's Castle after all.

Our luggage was in the hall waiting for us as John and I stood in the library with her, our coats on, taking one last look at the family tree on the wall.

"It's quite impressive," he said.

"Yes, it's real, all right. I just don't know if my branch of the family came from that mighty trunk." After a pause she added,

"Some of them were pretty horrible. As I have been. From time to time," she qualified.

"And what about Caroline?" I asked.

"She's my daughter, through and through. I don't know why I told such a whopper about her not being my child. Allan was too young to notice things properly. Both Vera and I were pregnant. Talk about a two-timing husband! I took Vera away until her child was born and she insisted on putting it up for adoption. It's what people did. I brought baby Caroline home. Who knows where that other child is now."

"Does it matter to you?" I asked.

"Sometimes I think about it and would like to know."

We were quiet as we looked at the preposterous family tree.

She turned, looking first to me and then to John with interest. "Do either of you write?"

"Not really," I answered cautiously while John was wisely silent.

"No matter. You can pick it up. I just thought of a wonderful plot line for my next book. Or series! The public may have lost interest in Alistair, but I think between the three of us, we could conjure up his long-lost son. Just think of the adventures the two of them could have together!"

I looked over her head at John in astonishment and a plea for help.

"Perhaps we'll talk another time," John said cheerfully, putting on his hat. "Patients to see in West Adams!"

I put my arm in his and added cheerfully and with relief, "And miles to go before we sleep!"

* * *

Reviews help readers discover my books, so leave a short line or two
on my
REVIEW PAGE
NEXT:

Aggie goes to Boston to help her cousin organize the last details of a charity debutante coming out party. Little do they know that what comes out are a series of scandals and a murder.

MURDER AT THE VALENTINE BALL

For more updates, check out my newsletter: www.Andreas-books.com